For Elaine

A Crowded Heart

Love,
Andrea McKenzie Raine xo

A Crowded Heart

A Prequel

by Andrea McKenzie Raine

INKWATER PRESS

PORTLAND • OREGON
INKWATERPRESS.COM

Scan this QR Code to learn more about this title

Copyright © 2016 by Andrea McKenzie Raine

Cover and interior design by Jayme Vincent
Cover images (bigstockphoto.com): The Setting Sun © Smileus; Military Dog Tags © 14ktgold

This is a work of fiction. The events described here are imaginary. The settings and characters are fictitious or used in a fictitious manner and do not represent specific places or living or dead people. Any resemblance is entirely coincidental.

All rights reserved. No part of this book may be reproduced or transmitted in any form or by any means whatsoever, including photocopying, recording or by any information storage and retrieval system, without written permission from the publisher and/or author. The views and opinions expressed in this book are those of the author(s) and do not necessarily reflect those of the publisher, and the publisher hereby disclaims any responsibility for them. Neither is the publisher responsible for the content or accuracy of the information provided in this document. Contact Inkwater Press at inkwater.com. 503.968.6777

Publisher: Inkwater Press | www.inkwaterpress.com

Paperback
ISBN-13 978-1-62901-313-8 | ISBN-10 1-62901-313-7

Kindle
ISBN-13 978-1-62901-314-5 | ISBN-10 1-62901-314-5

Printed in the U.S.A.

1 3 5 7 9 10 8 6 4 2

Chapter 1

WILLIS

Dieppe, France
August 1942

A rusty ceiling fan whirred lazily above like a helicopter propeller slowing down. The air was humid. Something was touching Willis' hand; another hand. He looked up to see a young nurse smiling at him.

"Welcome back, soldier," she said.

"Well, aren't you a sight for sore eyes," he said groggily. His throat was dry. "How long have I been asleep?"

"Quite a while, and rest is the best medicine. You've got a lot of healing to do after showing off on the battlefield like that," the nurse chirped. Willis winced at the bandage around his torso. He was beginning to recollect pieces of what had happened; the gunshots and the men falling around him. It had all gone so fast. He couldn't keep up with the blurred memories, vivid and chaotic. He was one of the lucky ones.

"Tell me, is being beautiful a prerequisite for nursing?"

"Ah. A sweet talker, eh? The girls told me I should watch out for you," she replied easily. "You had a few lucid moments."

"Don't listen to a word of it. I'm harmless."

"Hmmm, I'm not so sure about that. Wounded or not, I can tell you're a smooth one." Then she got off her chair and gave him a saucy parting look as she began to move on to the next poor sod lying on his hospital cot. She was a bright light in a gloomy room. Willis quickly pulled a cigarette out and asked the nurse if she could light him up. A kind nurse had left his pack beside his pillow.

"You do know that cigarettes are bad for your health," the nurse quipped.

"Yeah, I've heard they can kill you. I think I'll take my chances. Besides, there are worse vices," Willis responded. "The road of excess leads to the palace of wisdom."

"Is that right?" She smirked.

"You like that one? I've got more of them."

"I have no doubt. Actually, I was thinking that it could mean you finish living your cavalier life only to look back and realize what a bloody fool you are."

"Well, maybe," Willis mused. "What a party though!" When the nurse left his bedside, she was still smiling, although clearly unconvinced.

"Nice play, mate, but you're not going to get anywhere with that one." A British voice drifted over from the cot on his right. "No use chasing that skirt. Didn't you see the ring on her finger?"

"Yeah, well, I'm just trying to pass the time," Willis drawled. "So, when did you roll in?"

"I've had the privilege of listening to you snore for a few nights. You've been pretty out of it," the Brit replied. "I'm Sam." Sam deftly passed over his lighter, and Willis took it appreciatively.

"Ah, I see. Well, my apologies, Sam. I'm not sure how long I've been in this cot. I'm Willis. Judging by how many nurses have apparently visited me, I'd say I've been here for at least a week."

"Sounds like you spent a day at the beach too."

"Yeah, Blue Beach; I got more than a sunburn."

"We're the lucky ones, mate," Sam said solemnly.

"Where did you get hit?"

"That's a bit personal." Sam gave his new friend a side glance. Then he cleared his throat, sensing Willis' dry reaction. "We landed at Yellow Beach. My squadron was blindsided by the Krauts farther inland, about a day or so after the Dieppe Raid."

The tone of their conversation was flippant and nonchalant, but they both knew it was another kind of weapon: a shield to weather the chilling deeds they had witnessed and committed. They were soldiers, and all branded as though part of a secret club. The people at home would never understand. Sam was a joker. He liked to rib others, and often got close to touching a nerve, but he was not malicious. Sam lightened Willis' spirits; though, he did have to remind his new friend to go easy on the wisecracks or he might crack a rib. Willis was glad for the company. After a day or two, the nurses were visibly rolling their eyes when visiting the two men's cots, and they told the men they were "in cahoots." The young men were handsome, and the nurses secretly enjoyed the innocent flirtations. Sam had been grazed by a bullet on his right arm and was healing quickly. He expected to be sent back into the fight soon. Willis would be laid up for a longer time, but he hoped he wouldn't be sent home. He dreaded the idea. One afternoon, while they were having a quick poker game of Jacks Back, Willis asked his friend, "So, do you have a girl back home?"

Sam raised an eyebrow. "No one serious. I've got more wild oats to sow, you know? How about you?"

"No," Willis said flatly. "Having a girl at home would just make it harder being over here. It's better to not have any distractions." Sam nodded sternly while studying his cards.

"Yeah, it's good to keep your head clear," he began. "Still, a girl in your head can keep a little kindling in your chest; kind of like hope."

Sam ended up having the upper hand in the game, and Willis silently collected the cards and patted them back in the box. The two men didn't talk about anything too real; they didn't divulge too much information about themselves or who they were before the war. They kept their conversations light, enjoying the short reprieve from enemy fire. They knew they were as permanent as dew on the grass. Their odds of having a full house in poker were better than the chance of seeing the day through. After another week, Sam was discharged. Their encounter was brief, but his sudden absence was jarring. Another soldier was swiftly brought into Sam's cot. He had a bandage over his eye and didn't like to chat. Willis stopped flirting with the nurses, and they noticed his sullen disposition. One night, he had a vivid dream about going home on leave:

Willis stepped off the train in Vancouver and saw his parents and older sister standing on the platform. They looked nervous and rigid. His mother approached him first and straightened his tie. She didn't embrace him right away, as though she knew he might soon be a ghost; he wasn't home for good yet. His father stepped forward and shook his hand, welcoming him home, while his sister stood back, looking sober. His parents had been upset that he enlisted in the Canadian forces when the war broke out. They were one of the few families who felt that this was not their war and couldn't bear sending their own boys overseas to meet their end. The battle hadn't touched their shores and they didn't want to bring it into their homes.

Then his family was sitting in the kitchen at his parents' house, and his mother immediately began boiling water in a kettle on the stove and neatly placing rationed cookies on a serving tray, along with delicate cups, matching saucers, an heirloom sugar bowl, and a small sterling silver spoon. They had no notion of where he had been, and the only effects of war that kept them awake at night were the shortage of groceries.

"One cube or two, dear?" his mother asked calmly. "It's been so long, I'm afraid I don't remember."

"One is fine, Mother," Willis answered. He hadn't had sugar in ages and was concerned that more than one serving would send him into a fit.

"How are the boys holding up over there?" his father shot through the awkward niceties. Was it a sincere question, or was he digging just enough below the surface to find some place to stick his finger? Willis decided to give him the benefit of the doubt, to open up the communication with honesty and not try to sugarcoat the situation.

"Some days are good, Father. Most days are insufferable, but some days are good. We've all lost a lot of good friends, good men."

"Boys," his father snorted. "They're just damn, fool-headed boys."

"Not anymore," Willis shot back. His mother came over to the table, holding the tea tray and looking agitated. She passed Willis his teacup and gave him a wary look that said, "Please don't upset your father." She passed teacups to her husband and Ivy as well. Willis looked away and silently drank his tea. His father worked at the mill and was also lamenting all of the young boys who were leaving to fight. In his mind, they should stay home and help their town's economy and growth. He believed the war was robbing them all of their livelihood and family structure, shaking the core of their quiet existence. He didn't see the war as a tsunami that had to be stopped; instead, he only saw all the young men flying out of the nest to fight someone else's battles.

"So, Ivy." Willis turned his attention to his sister, who was watching them all with her swift eyes. She was nearly thirty years old, unmarried and still living at home. She tensed, as though he had poked her with a stick. "Any suitors come around?" Her eyes turned deadly, and then she looked down at her tea cup and saucer as though she were about to cry.

"Willis!" His mother snapped and rushed to Ivy's aide. "There are hardly any good men around here. As you say, they've all gone to fight that stupid war. Even the husbands leaving behind their poor wives and wee ones—and for what?"

"Well, the war got rid of the Depression, didn't it? Women are finally allowed out of the kitchen to help fight for the greater good, too. Besides, don't worry, Mother. Once the boys come marching back home, they'll all be clamouring up the side of your house to get into Ivy's ... room." He looked at Ivy pointedly, smirking. His sister's cheeks drained and then flushed a deep red. "Speaking of rooms," he continued, "I believe I will retire to mine. It's been a long trip and I'd like to unload my things."

"Certainly," his mother answered with an icy voice. His father peered at him over his newspaper. He left the room casually, knowing all eyes were on him. Once he was upstairs, he softly closed the door behind him until the latch clicked and then rolled the weight of his kit off his indented shoulder and onto the floral bed. He looked slowly around the small room, taking in the dainty flowers that plastered the four walls. This was his room once, with blue-striped wallpaper and cowboy bedding. Strangely, the fact that his mother had reclaimed it didn't faze him. Once he had put on the army attire, boarded the train, and left, she probably didn't imagine he would come back. He knew that his parents didn't want to acknowledge the war or him being part of it. She wasn't one to live in the past or hold on to false dreams. His family was different from everyone, and he was different from them. He harboured a deep sense of disconnect from his family and place of origin. They were full of contradictions, constantly concerned with fitting in socially, but having different ideas about the world. Willis saw them as armchair philosophers who hadn't seen much of the world, as far as he knew. Suddenly, he wished to be back with the other boys: wallowing in the dirt or keeping the rain off in the make-shift shanties, enveloped in cigarette smoke, playing cards, cradling a gun, and counting the days.

The window was cracked open, letting in the spring breeze, which lifted the lace curtains like the flirtation of a girl's skirt. Only his mind wasn't on girls. He was too distracted by the surreal calm, clean, picturesque surroundings. Glancing out the window, he saw a freshly cut lawn and white backyard fence. Still, his mind could only see blood on the grass and the dead bodies of young men hanging from the pickets. The clouds rolled by lazily in the blue sky. A woodpecker beat its head on a nearby tree. Willis blinked, turned away from the window, and opened his kit bag. His life was efficiently rolled up in there, in solid, neutral colours.

Willis breathed deeply as he slowly surfaced from the dream; he wasn't entirely convinced that he hadn't transported himself back there in the present time. His parents' influence had managed to become imbedded in his brain; it seemed he could feel them, even from this great distance. He remembered how angry, worried, and disappointed his parents were when he announced that he had enlisted. In return, he was frustrated that they couldn't see the bigger picture. He wasn't entirely sure how much of it was true and how much he had conjured up in his mind about them.

He also vaguely recalled how his mother had set up visitations for him with various local girls before he had announced he was going to Europe to fight the enemy. Perhaps she sensed the war coming and the restlessness in him. The handful of girls who came over for a simple chat and a cup of tea were pretty enough, but there wasn't much going on underneath the carefully set curls on their heads. Whenever he tried to talk to them about something serious, like politics or where they thought the world was headed, they would just shrug their shoulders nervously and twitter something incoherent. He noticed acutely how some of them made their tea cups vibrate slightly at such questions, while he ignored the angry glares from his mother, who was always seated across the room. She was an observer and he was a captive, or so she thought. In reality, he was the one conducting the social experiment. Usually, he would gulp back his tea and unceremoniously leave the room, saying he had to return to a book he was engrossed in. From the safety of the upstairs landing, he would then hear his mother apologizing profusely to the young, dimwitted doe for her son's rudeness. The door would close soundly, but she never came after him; she never reproached him. Maybe she was afraid of him too. She couldn't comprehend him, and after the third or fourth attempt to find him a life companion (or at the very least, a female distraction), she gave up and never mentioned it again. Perhaps she was beginning to think he didn't like girls. It didn't bother him; he simply didn't want her meddling in his life, and he knew he had a much more important path to pursue; he couldn't put his finger on it yet, but he knew something much larger was coming.

The war was a blessing to him, a way out. He shuddered at the idea of being tied down for life with someone whom he could barely hold a conversation. He didn't like the idea of feeling obliged to stay in his hometown for any reason. All of the mothers in the area were trying to get their sons and daughters together to secure a future: the promise of continuing their familial lines, boosting the population, and increasing industry. Everyone had known they were on the brink of war, and the threat of losing so many young men was too overwhelming to talk about. It seemed only the old men and politicians had openly discussed the notion of going to war, those who were too old to worry about the ramifications or too closely linked to the unfolding events to ignore the possibility. The headlines were printed concerning what was happening "over there." It hung in the air, and they were all breathing it in and out for the longest time. Now everyone stood in their kitchens or sat in their reading chairs, helpless. They were all watching it come, waiting for it to hit their shore.

"Do you think I'll be sent home?" Willis eventually asked the nurse as she put a new dressing on his wound. She sensed the apprehension in his voice and was surprised he didn't sound more hopeful.

"No, love, you're not too bad off. I'll double-check with the doctor, but I think we might keep you around for the entertainment." She winked and squeezed his wrist. He blew out a wisp of air, closed his eyes, and drifted to sleep.

EINDHOVEN, HOLLAND
SEPTEMBER 18, 1944

Willis sat at the small café table with his squadron, soaking up the end-of-summer sunshine and nursing his dark beer. The streets were wild with people celebrating, dancing in their vibrant native colours and embracing each other. Willis vaguely listened to the other young men swap stories about their lives before the war and the girls who were waiting for them. He didn't chime in; instead, he just sat and listened with an odd, satisfied little smile on his face. The liberation of South Holland was a significant victory, and there was a strong vibration in the air of the possibility of the war ending soon. Still, this precious time was a mini-break, a reprieve from the life existing on the war front that carried on. They were a lucky few held in a place of sanctuary for a brief spell—a place to regroup, rejuvenate, and enjoy a small yet historical victory, but not forget the responsibilities that lay ahead. They couldn't hear the gunshots and bombs, or the planes plummeting to the ground, but it was still happening. They were also all quietly mourning the resounding failure of Operation Market Garden and trying to savour this victory, and future victories; every swipe at the Germans was a greater niche forged in the foundation of tyranny. The men didn't relay any battle stories or mention any of the fallen soldiers. Despite the near autumn chill, they all drank, laughed loudly, and danced in the street with the local people, grateful. Today they were still alive. Willis' ear turned away from the superficial chatter at the table, and his eye caught sight of a familiar soldier sitting at another table across the square.

"Excuse me, fellows," he said absentmindedly. He picked up his beer and strolled over to a table filled with British soldiers. He recognized their uniforms—they were Commando, special operations; light infantry. As he approached, a couple of the men casually turned their heads and acknowledged him as their laughter from the humorous anecdote someone had shared died down.

"Hey, a Canuck!" one of the men greeted him, easily recognizing his beret. "Pull up a chair!" It wasn't the man Willis had first spied; that man sat across the table gulping down a pint of beer. Then he looked up at Willis, wiped his mouth slowly, and said, "Say, mate, I know you! You're that smooth-talking soldier who injured his funny bone!"

"Willis." He smiled broadly and extended his hand, reaching over the table and parting the group.

"That's right," the other man said. "Sam!" Then Sam began to relay the story to his buddies about the days they spent as bedmates in the military hospital. "Willis here is a hound. He flirted with anyone who was wearing a skirt." He winked devilishly. "I've got your number, mate."

"Well, everybody needs a pastime, eh? Besides, it keeps your blood pumping."

"Best pastime I can think of," Sam agreed, and they clinked beer steins.

There was talk of the war winding down, even though the battles raged on. There had been talk of the war ending for months, even years. Everyone was tired, and the allies seemed to have the upper hand for the moment. The liberation of Holland was a pivotal event that was sure to force the Nazis to buckle. Willis tried to push the war far from his thoughts as he sat with his new army buddies in a café in Eindhoven. Strange, this was the one place in Europe the war wasn't happening anymore, and yet, clearly, it was affecting everyone. It was near-autumn and there were small birds searching for scraps under the tables. Once again, Willis tried to focus on being in the moment, in this place. He watched his buddies swallow their beer in the afternoon sunlight, talk about their girls at home, and burst into wartime choruses. They could have been on holiday. In a way, they were.

Willis finished his beer, and almost as soon as he placed his empty mug on the table, a young barmaid appeared and asked him in her best English if he cared for another. The pitcher was low. The sun behind her created a halo silhouette around her light brown pin curls. She had a plain, bright face.

"*Danke*," he answered. He could detect her faint German accent and visibly squirmed in his seat. How was it that she was here?

"The same?" she asked.

"*Bitte*," he replied. He had an edge to his voice. She gave him a small, close-mouthed smile and disappeared into the café with his empty stein. His friends were too drunk to notice their conversation, as though he and this girl had managed to step out of time.

"Hey, Willis, why didn't you order a pitcher for us?" Sam asked as soon as the girl was out of earshot.

"Because she asked me, not you," Willis answered smugly. A few moments later, the young girl returned with a clean stein and a fresh pitcher. She turned toward Willis and gave him a secret wink as she set the stein down in front of him. Then she went back inside the café.

"Oh, Romeo, too bad," Sam exclaimed from across the table. "I guess she wasn't just trying to get into your army gear after all!"

"Oh, grow up," Willis muttered. Sam was a couple of years younger than the other men. His natural sense of humour helped shield his insecurities and anxiety about his lack of worldly experience, which included women.

Willis poured another beer and took a long swallow to hide his smile while his new friends jostled him. They were a bunch of young yahoos, but they were all lucky to be alive. The British troops' captain came around and reminded them that they would be heading back up to the camp soon. They had orders to roll out in the morning. The men didn't have to meet curfew right away, but the young captain was taking a head count of his soldiers and making sure they were all staying in line and not getting too rowdy.

"Aye, aye, captain," a few of the soldiers mocked him and gave half-hearted salutes to his shrinking back as the older boy moved down the road. They were all boys. They did like their captain, and they knew he was doing his best and not having an easy time; they simply all hated their uniforms.

"Are we ready to march up to our bunks?" one of Willis' friends asked the group once the pitcher was emptied into their gullets and they began to leave the table, settling the tab and pushing in their chairs. Willis craned his neck to see inside the café door.

He could see the back of the young barmaid's head as she spoke with another girl. Then she came out with a cloth in her hand and demurely bent over a table with a swift motion. Another girl came out to chat with her briefly, and then disappeared back inside. He wasn't sure if he should approach her now or wait until she was finished working. He decided he couldn't wait. He moved in slow and casual, as though he would pass the café altogether and then veered over to speak to her.

"Thank you for bringing out the fresh pitcher earlier," he said. It was the best conversation starter he could think of because he was nervous. He didn't want to seem nervous and silently berated himself. She looked up from the table with a distracted frown. Then, when she saw him, her face eased into a pleasant shyness that he liked.

"You are welcome," she said. "Your friends looked thirsty too."

He laughed, "They were. That was very kind."

"It is my job." She smiled and turned her attention back to wiping the tables. Her friend came outside again to check on her and flashed him a suspicious look. Then she crooked an eyebrow in amusement. "Frieda, come inside for your share of the tips," she said and swung her hips a little more when she left.

"I'll be right there," Frieda answered. She looked at Willis apologetically. "I have to go."

"Me too," he said. "But I wondered if I could talk with you for a while after your work is finished."

"Sure," she said. She balled the cloth in her hand and went inside the café. She left the door open. He had placed his beret on his head and swiftly turned to follow the other boys up the road. His cheeks were pink.

———◆◆◆———

An hour later, Willis lay on his makeshift bunk after organizing his gear.

"When is curfew?" he asked another boy in the shelter.

"Eight o'clock. Why? Are you going to go into town?"

"It's six o'clock now; I've got time to look around," Willis answered absently.

"You want some company?" The other boy sounded eager. He was propped up on his pillow with a girly magazine.

"No, thanks," Willis said. The other boy narrowed his eyes at him, although Willis didn't notice. He was busy tying his shiny army-issued shoes. "I'll be back soon."

"See you," the other boy said, dejected. The evening sky was still light. Willis found he was bouncing down the road. He wasn't even sure what he would find, or if she would still be there. As he neared the quaint sidewalk café, he could see the other girls moving the chairs inside. Willis waited outside the café with the glow of sunset behind him. Finally, Frieda stepped out. She was wearing a yellow dress with small red polka dots. He hadn't noticed her dress before, because her apron covered it. Her hair was loose. She had a small bounce in her step that made him more nervous—as though she were a young lion cub bounding toward him without any notion of potential danger.

"Hello!" she said spritely.

"Hello." Willis smiled. His hands were in his pockets. He wasn't really sure about what he was doing there or why he had to see her. He turned and offered his arm, and she took it easily. They began walking with no destination in mind. He vaguely thought he would let her lead, since she knew the city better than he did.

"So, you are a soldier?" she asked. The question was almost rhetorical, but she left enough silence for him to give an answer.

"Yes," he said simply.

"You do not have the same accent as your friends. Are you American?"

"Canadian," he was quick to correct her.

"Ah," she said. "You already know I am German," she said matter-of-factly. He stopped and looked at her. He wasn't sure how to respond. He didn't want to say he was sorry. He was afraid it might come out wrong.

"Yes," he said. "I should have thought before I spoke."

"It's alright." She shrugged and smiled a small smile. "My father is an ex-patriot of Germany and my mother is Dutch. I grew up here. I have German in my blood, but that is all. The war is bad for everyone. I want you to stop Hitler." He put his hand over her smaller hand, which was tucked inside his arm.

"The war should be over soon," he said. Frieda didn't say anything, and they kept walking.

"Where will you go next?" she finally asked him.

"I don't know ... wherever we are needed most."

"Are you afraid?" Her question was so straightforward it startled him. He rarely allowed himself to dwell on his fears.

"A little, I suppose, but I don't have much choice. I chose to come and fight. Who knows, it may all be over before we even receive our next orders." He was making a wish out loud.

"You are a brave man," she said thoughtfully. He smiled, feeling his cheeks flush. "When do you leave?"

"Tomorrow," he replied. He felt his stomach sink. She nodded, unconsciously tightening her grip on his arm. He felt it, but said nothing.

"What will you do when you go home?"

"Go home?"

"Yes, after the war?" It seemed, in her eyes, death was not an option for him. He felt a surge of reassurance. Again, he had rarely allowed himself to think of it, but he did have a plan that he kept hidden in his heart.

"I think I'd like to become a lawyer," he said softly. If he spoke the words too loudly or confidently, fate may hear him and he might be stricken dead tomorrow. There were already too many young men who could no longer dream of home. They had some space to dream now that this small piece of the world had been reclaimed from Hitler's grasp. It was one brick removed from the ominous wall, weakening its grey, foreboding structure and threatening it to collapse into rubble.

"I think you will be a fine lawyer," she said. "You seem solid and honest to me." The sun had set behind the buildings, and there were fewer people on the sidewalks.

"I should get back for curfew," he said regretfully. "Where are you staying?"

She smiled sheepishly. "I've been walking us toward my apartment. I live just around the corner. You go; I can see myself home."

Willis felt a bit torn, but he sensed that she wanted to say goodbye here, before she turned the corner and into his memory.

"Would it be alright if I kissed you goodbye?" The right corner of her lips turned up in answer. He leaned down and touched them with his lips, gently at first, and then her lips parted and embraced his mouth. She tasted like summer and all things ephemeral.

Chapter 2

That night Willis slept dreaming only of a young girl in a yellow dress with red polka dots. The next morning, Willis spotted Sam at the train station. All of the troops were rallied together. Willis wasn't able to get close to his friend, but he did make eye contact, and they informally saluted each other. Sam's train was ready for boarding, and Willis watched as his friend moved farther away into the sea of uniforms. Shortly afterwards, Willis' squadron began to board their own appointed train. Sam's train was still waiting in the station, and Willis noticed some kerfuffle stirring with the train workers. Sam's train had mechanical problems and was shut down for maintenance, so his squadron ended up boarding Willis' train instead. They were all heading to the same destination. Sam found Willis on the train and persuaded his seat companion to move somewhere else. Once Sam got settled in his seat, he wouldn't stop jibing Willis about his quiet smile, which revealed nothing, while they rode the train to their next uncertainty. As much as Willis pretended to be slightly annoyed, he was secretly glad for the distraction of having his friend with him. They were being sent to the Battle of Scheldt to assist in opening the port of Antwerp to allow shipping supplies for the allied front. Sam was convinced that Willis had lost his timely virginity to the café girl, who, in his memory, batted her eyelashes at him. He wanted every perverse detail, but Willis wouldn't crack. Frieda was special, and he wouldn't let her become a cheap locker room story.

"Remember, soldier, you are still going into battle."

"She'll get me through it," he said. Sam shook his head, slightly concerned.

"Sounds to me like we've already lost you forever," Sam mused.

Willis' smile did eventually diminish as he thought about his duty once again, which took precedence. He found himself packed in with the other men; all of them trying to keep their hope alive by the light at the end of their cigarettes. Throughout the war, he had tried to find something beautiful in the flares and grenade explosions that lit up the night sky, forgetting how they signified revenge and death. Even now, with the damp fear seeping in, Willis kept the brief memory of Frieda burning in his chest, a small flame to create enough light to keep him warm. After the liberation of southern Holland, in his foolish heart, he believed they may be able to wait out the war from a relatively safe standpoint. Instead, they were still fighting to take the kneecaps out of the Nazi regime.

When the soldiers reached their destination and reported for duty, they were informed that Eindhoven had been bombed by the Germans that afternoon. The number of casualties, including soldiers and civilians, was devastating. Willis felt his knees start to buckle, but he managed to stay standing. Sam could see the colour drain out of his face. The memory of celebration was fresh in their minds, and the idea that it had all been turned to rubble in a matter of hours was sickening. They were silent for two minutes, and during that time, Willis could only think of Frieda.

Sam and Willis stuck close to each other during the five grueling weeks that ensued in Scheldt. Finally, the port was cleared. After the dedicated and costly efforts of the Western allies, Willis hoped this would mean the beginning of the end, but he knew deep down that the end was not yet in sight. A runaway train couldn't be expected to stop on a dime. The dust had not yet settled, and they were being rounded up and deployed to their next endpoint.

SAM

Sam was like a turtle; he had a soft, vulnerable heart and deep insecurities that were heavily shielded by his humour, cockiness, and false bravado. He was the youngest in his family and grew up with four sisters who doted on him. As he was growing up, he watched his sisters and how they interacted with the world; it was complicated, and they seemed to develop split personalities to adjust to the changing landscapes and dynamics of their female lives. He didn't understand at all. As a result, women became intimidating alien creatures that made him feel awkward, incapable, and childlike. He also quickly realized he had no physical attraction to them. He was more drawn to men because he could relate to them; men were simple, logical, and primal. The grey area that existed in a man's world was marginal compared to the planet women seemed to inhabit and endure. He was still young and hadn't completely come into his own skin yet. He sensed worldliness about Willis; there was a bright light in him, which served as a beacon. Sam felt more comfortable and optimistic when he was with him.

During the Battle of Scheldt, Sam's unit lost their young, determined, and good-natured captain. In the wake of the loss, Sam took on the acting role of captain, as he was the closest in rank, and no one debated his authority. He was also determined to keep up the morale of the men after their hard blow. Everyone liked Sam;

he was able to maintain the voice of reason and had an endearing quality about him. He even managed to joke with the young men about how he wasn't very proficient in letter writing and didn't want to be put in the awkward position of potentially embarrassing anyone by accidentally writing to their families about how their son had or had not died as a virgin. "So, none of you lot better die on me!" Sam half-scolded them. There were snorts and small chuckles and red faces all around, but the boys got the message. For the most part, the men took heed; only a few boxes draped in national flags were sent home, along with solemn salutes and formal letters.

In November 1944, Sam was sent to fight in Operation Clipper in Germany, while Willis was sent to France to assist in clearing the Channel coast. While the hypnotic, relentless workings of the train wheels rumbled beneath him, Sam felt a strange calm, as though he were invincible now. He had survived nearly everything the war could throw at him, and the memory of each battle was growing over like scar tissue: a second skin.

Chapter 3

After the respective battles ended, the men who were still standing were granted a short leave in London. Willis partly wished he could go home to see his parents. Writing home was difficult, as the letters took weeks or months to be delivered. He imagined their worry, watching for strange black cars pulling into the driveway. Instead, Willis was forced to stay close to the war, to his duty and promise. He could only hope his parents had learned to be proud of him.

Stepping onto British soil was like taking in a breath of fresh air, and the young men had a full week to breathe it in. As soon as he and the other men from his troop got off the train at Victoria Station, they parted ways to wander the city. Although everyone was living in the shadow of the war, life continued. The British people didn't seem afraid to be in the streets and live their daily lives. Willis strolled down the uneven roads, smiling at the passersby, especially the young women, who blushed and tittered at the sight of his smart uniform. He stepped into a pub where he found a group of rowdy soldiers in the back corner, and immediately Willis recognized them—he strolled over and grabbed a couple of chairs while one of the men was relaying a humorous tale to his mates. It was Sam. As the men laughed uproariously, Sam caught Willis' eye. He stood up and pulled his friend into a one-armed hug, patting him on the back. After a while, the other men, who were finishing their third pitcher, stood up to settle their tabs and leave. Willis and Sam took over a smaller table, and a waitress came by momentarily; they each ordered a pint of dark ale.

"We made it through again." Sam casually said. Then he added more somberly, "Do you think it is true what everyone is saying—that it shouldn't be too long now before it's all over?"

"I damn well hope so. After Holland, I don't think the Nazis have a leg to stand on. I think we helped take the bricks out from the bottom, and that was the big push that will send Hitler back to the other side of the sandbox," Willis replied.

"Do you still think about that filly in Eindhoven?" Sam asked.

Willis gave his friend a sideways glance. "Now and then, but I try not to—don't even know if she made it through the bombing. I hope so." He frowned. "Either way, it's doubtful I'll ever see her again, but it's nice to have a warm thought."

"It's a good thing to keep a fire going in the back; just remember to keep moving forward too," Sam said. The waitress placed their pints on the table.

"My, aren't *you* the philosopher?"

"Well, aren't *you* the romantic? You can think with your heart, mate—I prefer to use my head," Sam said and began drinking his beer.

"Who says I'm not using my head?" Willis asked indignantly. Sam was about to retort with *which one?* However, he thought better of it and decided to raise his glass to his friend instead. The truth was he desperately wished he had someone to warm his thoughts and get him through the fear and loneliness. He felt a pang of envy, but he didn't want to snuff out his friend's hopeful spark.

After a while, Willis parted company with Sam, so they could both explore the city untethered. They agreed to meet up again later. Eventually, Willis decided to browse in a little bookstore that caught his eye. The bookstore was two-level, and he scanned the poetry section downstairs: Keats, Burns, Coleridge, and Wordsworth, to name a few. He found a few favourites in the collections, such as *The Rime of the Ancient Mariner*, *Tintern Abbey*, and *A Red, Red Rose*. He enjoyed the traditional poets and was not yet ready for the modern spouting of Kipling and Pound. There was passion in the voices of the older poets, but not so much rebellion. He placed Wordsworth carefully back on the shelf, imagining a life of roaming the countryside with a mind full of free thoughts. He didn't buy a copy. Instead, he let the words resonate in his head. He climbed the staircase to the second level—the arts and fiction section. Almost as soon as he reached the landing, he spotted a blonde-haired woman in the Arts aisle. She was engrossed in a book of Van Gogh prints, and he watched her as she absentmindedly tucked a golden strand of hair behind her ear. She wore a white cardigan sweater and brown, knee-length skirt. Her hair had been set in careful pin curls, as was the fashion. She was young, fresh, and pretty. He moved toward her like a hunter approaching a doe, and she didn't acknowledge him until he was nearly right on top of her. She raised her eyes from her book and slightly jumped.

"Would you recommend Van Gogh?" he asked casually. He lazily fingered a book spine on the shelf beside him, looking vaguely interested in the selection of titles.

"Who in their right mind wouldn't? Van Gogh was a fascinating individual and artist," she answered easily. It was clear that her nerves had settled from being approached by a young, handsome stranger in uniform.

"Aren't all artists fascinating?" he asked. He seemed to be challenging her. *How forward*, she thought, but smiled in spite of herself.

"Yes, I suppose they are. Artists manage to find some beauty in everything," she answered.

"You sound like you're an expert," he said.

"I am an art student at Cambridge. I'm studying art history." She had a certain bravado about her that he liked.

"So you don't live in London?"

"No, not anymore. I'm visiting my parents."

"I see. How long are you in London?"

"Until the New Year. I've been here for a week already."

"Oh, right."

"How long are you staying, soldier?" she was feeling braver.

"One week. We arrived today." Then he had a thought. "Can I purchase your copy of Van Gogh for you?"

"Oh, thank you," she accepted. They walked to the cashier, and Willis unfolded a few pound notes from his pocket. He had exchanged his leave allowance money at the train station. Once they were on the sidewalk outside the bookstore, he didn't know where to take her. He felt a wave of déjà vu wash over him.

"Why don't you walk me home?" she suggested.

"Is it far?" he asked, worried that he would get lost on his first day in the big city of London. She laughed at him.

"Not very," she assured him. "My parents live beside Kensington Park." The location sounded posh.

"Okay, let's go." The day was clear, and when they reached Kensington Park, after a time and a lengthy discussion about her studies at Cambridge and his life in the military, he led her into the park to sit on a bench for a while.

"Would it be alright if I saw you again before I leave?" he asked timidly.

"I would like to see you again," she answered. "Perhaps you could come in the evening and meet my parents." He wasn't entirely prepared to meet her parents, but he agreed. Maybe she needed permission from her parents to be accompanied by a strange, young soldier. He offered to come by the next evening. Then he walked her to the lavish townhouse complex next to the park. It was close to tea time. He squeezed her hand and said goodnight.

"My name is Ellie," she said. After all of their walking and talking, he hadn't asked her.

"Willis," he said. His voice sounded serious, which surprised him.

The next evening, after spending a day wandering around London on a self-guided tour, he found himself back on the front step of her parents' house. When Willis rang the doorbell, he could hear the classical chime echo in the front hall. The front door opened, and there stood an older gentleman in a formal tuxedo. Willis was about to address the man as Ellie's father when he heard another male voice in the next room.

"Thank you, Frederick," the other man boomed and promptly appeared in the doorway. "I am Ellie's father, Mr. Birch." He extended his hand. Willis shook it readily and introduced himself.

"Come in, sir," the older man stepped back so that Willis could enter. "Would you care for a drink?" Ellie's father was already well into his glass of scotch, looking relaxed.

"A brandy, please," Willis answered. Mr. Birch pursed his lips in approval and motioned Willis into the sitting room. Frederick bowed and disappeared quietly. Ellie's mother was sitting primly on a chaise lounge just inside the arched doorway. She turned and smiled at Willis with her eyes. She didn't stand up, but extended her slim arm toward him. He took her hand and bowed slightly and acknowledged her as Mrs. Birch. He was not sure whether she expected him to kiss her pale knuckles. He couldn't see how she would expect such a gesture on a first meeting.

"Nice to meet you, Willis," she said. She didn't seem offended at all, which relieved him. His gaze then fell on Ellie, who was seated at the far side of the room, which was painted a soft, inviting yellow, not a cool blue or intense and foreboding red. He felt comfortable there.

"And, of course, you know our Ellie," Mr. Birch boomed again.

"Yes, a little," Willis found himself saying. Ellie smiled at him encouragingly.

"Here, sit down." Her mother motioned toward an armchair that was situated across from her, diagonal to Ellie's chair. He felt as though they were all chess pieces waiting for someone to make the next move. There was a formality there, but it was subtle and underlying. Frederick reappeared with Willis' brandy—two fingers deep.

"Ellie tells us you are with the Canadian troops," Ellie's mother began.

"Yes, the First Canadian Army," he answered. "I was raised near Vancouver—that's on the west coast." His throat felt dry, so he took a sip of his drink.

"Were you drafted?" Ellie's father asked.

"I signed up as soon as I could," Willis answered.

"Good man," her father nodded. Willis didn't want to talk too much about the war. Other than the higher politics governing the war, it was a dreary subject. He had seen much more than he needed to, but he wouldn't allow the experience to bury itself under his skin.

"What will you do after the war?" Mrs. Birch asked him kindly. It seemed that she didn't want to hear about his gory tales either, and he was grateful. They understood. Everyone read the papers.

"I would like to pursue a career in law," he said. He sat up straighter as he spoke, and his voice held conviction.

"Police work?"

"No, I would like to become a lawyer."

"A fine profession, Mr.—" Mr. Birch trailed off as he realized he had never learned Willis' last name.

"Hancocks," Willis interjected.

"... Mr. Hancocks. And a solid name to match your profession."

Ellie sat beaming as her parents exchanged knowing looks of approval. Willis sipped his brandy.

"So, will you pursue your career in Canada?" Mrs. Birch asked. The question carried more weight, and Ellie looked anxious for a moment.

"Mother," Ellie breathed. Her cheeks flushed.

"No, it's alright," Willis said. "I don't know. I don't think so—I mean, if the war ends in our favour. Well, I've grown accustomed to being over here. I believe I would like to stay."

"Cambridge has a fine law program," Mr. Birch ventured. "And our Ellie can attest to the quality of the instructors, not to mention the campus grounds." Ellie blushed deeper.

"Sounds marvelous." Willis smiled. Ellie gave him a mixed look of happiness and caution, as though she didn't dare allow herself to hope. Perhaps he was simply trying to make a good impression with her parents. Perhaps he felt cornered. He then smiled a smile that was only meant for her, which lit her up and scared her all at once.

"Our Ellie will have a successful career also," Mr. Birch spoke over the glance between the two, "as an art gallery owner or a museum curator or an artist in her own right."

"I have no doubts," Willis responded, and he began talking to her parents about her art studies. In turn, her parents boasted about what an expert she had become on the subject of art and the success of her modest paintings and sketches. As the evening drew to a close and Willis was becoming increasingly aware of his curfew, he was preparing himself to formally ask to continue seeing Ellie while he was in London and maintaining contact after he left. In the end, there was no need. Her father simply shook his hand and told him he was welcome to come by their house at any time. Mr. Birch even went so far as to say he hoped Willis would entertain Ellie during his stay in London.

"If she will allow me," Willis answered, grinning. Ellie looked as though she were ready to jump out of her shoes. The older couple left them to say goodnight at the front door. "Would you like me to come by and entertain you tomorrow?" he asked in low tones.

"Oh, please do," she giggled. He squeezed both of her hands and kissed her on the cheek.

"Until tomorrow," he said.

"Goodnight," she said, smiling.

A Crowded Heart

During Willis' week-long stay in London, he spent the majority of his time with Ellie. Enough time to silence Sam about the girl in Eindhoven.

"You seem to find a girl in every port" was the only sidelong comment from Sam, and Willis only winked at him. Sam sensed something different in his friend's demeanour, though—something with substance. He was decidedly happy for his friend and kept silent, although he couldn't resist slapping Willis on the back from time to time. Sam wasn't too surprised, then, when Willis pulled him aside and showed him a sparkling promise ring he intended to give to Ellie before he returned to finish the war.

Chapter 4

Sam fought hard to keep back the words that were banging on the back of his teeth—"What if you don't live through the war?" Then he realized this fear belonged to him alone, and he would only be projecting his own worry. He was sure Willis had considered everything and he didn't want to straighten the hopeful, enduring smile on his friend's lips.

"Today is the day," Willis announced to Sam on their last day of leave. "I'm going to give her the ring and ask her to wait for me." He wasn't asking her to marry him yet, at least not officially. He knew there was no guarantee he would come back. This would be a safer engagement, a way of leaving a window open. The men were scheduled to board the train back to France in the evening.

"Go get her." Sam winked at him.

The morning clouds were threatening rain as Willis hopped on the double-decker bus headed toward Kensington Park. Ellie looked sunny, as always. He smiled broadly and felt his heart thump in his chest when he came up the street and saw her standing in front of her parents' townhouse, eagerly watching for him.

"Where are you taking me today?" she asked happily.

"You'll see." He smiled at her.

"You're always full of surprises." She shook her blonde head, laughing. Her eyes held the universe in them. He led her down the street to the bus stop with a secret smile plastered on his face. Small drops of rain began falling on them, and neither one of them had thought to bring a brolly. Ellie put her hand out to feel the wet on her fingers.

"Oh dear," she giggled, and Willis pulled her in tight beside him. The rough material of his army jacket and the comfort of his arm kept her dry. When the bus finally came, the spitting rain was beginning to come down in buckets and they scrambled into the lower level of the bus.

"At least you have a hat!" she squealed, lightly patting the rain drops away from her tousled hair.

"You look beautiful," he replied, and he was quite serious. She stopped and looked at him softly, as though he weren't real. She then grasped his hand to make sure, still watching his eyes, and let go a little sigh. She didn't want to be brave, knowing this could be their last day. Instead, she changed the atmosphere by looking out the window, still wondering where they were going. The bus stopped at the National Art Gallery, and Willis pulled her out of her seat.

"This is us!" He grinned.

"The art gallery?" she asked. "But Willis, dear, the gallery is empty."

"What?"

"Yes, didn't you know? When the war began, the government decided to clear out all of the paintings to protect them. It was a good thing, too, after what happened during the Blitz."

Willis felt stupid and deflated. Sometimes he forgot about the war, and especially when he was with her. Still, the war was present and everywhere.

"We could see if there is a concert today," she suggested hopefully. "The gallery is still open to the public for concert entertainment—oh, they put on fine shows!"

"Alright, then," Willis brightened. "Let's go and see." Sure enough, inside the gallery people were bustling in the main area, chatting over their cups of tea and coffee and small cakes, and finding their seats, which were arranged in theatre style. The orchestra began to play the next piece as Ellie and Willis settled in. He watched her face as the music filled the room; she seemed to be less moved by the music and more intent on watching the musicians themselves. She was paying more attention to the artists than the art. He took her hand lightly from her lap and placed it on his thigh, holding on gently. She gave a ghost of a smile, her eyes looking ahead. There was already a familiarity between them, a kind of comfort. This growing love wasn't showy or wildly intense. Instead, this was sturdy and peaceful, and it made him happy. The set ended, and Willis turned to her.

"I leave tonight, Ellie," he said somberly.

"Yes, I know," she said. She wouldn't look at him. He squeezed her hand.

"I want to give you something," he continued. She turned her head toward him, her eyes last to follow. He reached into his pocket, and she held her breath. He gave her a small, square, velvet box.

She lifted the small box out of his hands and opened the lid. A simple ring with a small, pink, round diamond glinted at her. "It is not an engagement ring," he said, "not yet." Willis explained hastily. "I am hoping you will wait for me, Ellie. I'm giving you a promise." She wanted to ask him if he could promise to return to her, but instead, she bit the inside of her cheek. She wanted to hold on to his promise, whatever it meant. He was saying he loved her. For now, that was more than enough.

"Of course I'll wait for you, Willis," she whispered, holding back tears of joy and fright. He beamed at her and placed the ring on the slender ring finger of her left hand. She thought she might switch it to her right hand after he left. A part of her didn't want to be marked as his until the war was over and he was alive and home. They sat through the next set with their hands clasped and their minds lost in distraction.

Chapter 5

Willis returned to the front lines with Ellie's photograph in his breast pocket. She had given it to him as a parting gift before she kissed him goodbye on her parents' front steps. He thought about how he had wished they could spend one night together, but he didn't want to risk leaving her behind with more than a promise ring. He was young and scared, as much as he refused to admit to either strike against him. He didn't want to be foolish too. They would be together, and the thought of their future would bring him home safe. He also still had Sam's company for a while longer—to keep up his morale, slap him in the head, and cement his feet to the ground when needed.

Upon their return from leave, Willis and Sam were assigned to different posts. Sam was sent to Ardennes, France, to fight the Battle of the Bulge and Willis fought in northern Germany, marching up to Weser River.

December 1944

Dearest Ellie,

A month seems like a year being apart from you. I won't tell you where I am, because you will only worry. Besides, any place away from you is cold and dark. I am still in one piece, with all the pieces that matter attached. I will tell you my only regret is not having the chance to touch you, beyond a kiss, before I left. Still, the memory of your kiss keeps the fear out of me. I am not so afraid when I hear the violence and see the human damage in the lights in the sky; they are mere BB guns and fireworks to me. In my mind, the men only pretend to fall. My heart has already been pierced by a love-tipped arrow, which will prevent it from turning black. I am shielded, I think, for this brief while. I can only hope you have kept my ring, my token of intention, and that it is enough to keep me close in your thoughts. Bad timing, perhaps; it was all I could do, as my only fear now is to lose you. Strange, although I am careful to preserve myself for you, I don't worry so much anymore. I hope you are able to sleep well and that you aren't dwelling too much on my safety and whereabouts. I imagine you visiting with your family and friends, and I am grateful that you are far away from all of this insanity.

Keep well, love. I look forward to your handwriting—to reading your heart—and I will write again soon.

Yours,
Willis

Ellie received the letter one month later, handed to her by her mother. The younger woman opened the seal to first look at the date.

"Why must the mail correspondence be so painfully slow?" she asked, sighing deeply. She placed the letter gently in her skirt pocket and fled upstairs to read her lover's words in private. Her mother smiled after her and, folding her arms in front of her, turned away from the foot of the staircase.

Once safely inside her room, with the door closed, Ellie reopened the letter and read silently. Her heart tightened in her chest, and she was filled with a mixture of longing and indignation at his suggestion that they could have spent a night together before he left to fight. *What purpose would that have served?* He might have left her in trouble. Still, she couldn't deny that she had thought of him in that way too. She couldn't be cross with him. He was in a place that she couldn't bring herself to imagine, and he was reaching out to her for comfort. They would be together soon enough. Soon, they would have all the luxuries in the world. Solemnly, she folded the letter and placed it back in the envelope, tucking it away in her drawer. There she saw the small ring Willis had given her. She picked it up and caressed the silver between her fingers. She held it up to the sunlight coming through the tall window. Then she placed the ring carefully back in the small drawer. She was keeping the ring pure to wear for him, as much as she was keeping herself.

Ellie walked over to her writing desk in the corner of the brightly lit room, took out her scented stationary and fountain pen, and began to write.

January 1945

My Dearest,

I have just now received your letter and feel compelled to write you this instant. Since this is to be our only means of connection, other than the unseen strings of the heart, I want to keep our flow of conversation as consistent as possible. There is an obstacle of time, distance, and place between us. I was disheartened having to spend our first Christmas apart, but I was able to keep myself occupied with preparations for the holidays. I hope you are able to stay warm, wherever you are. I have enclosed some mistletoe with the hopes that you might save it for me and to let you know where I would like to be. I'm glad you are keeping my photograph close to you and private. After all, it is for you alone to look at—to think about home and better days ... and me.

We have snow here. I watch the neighbourhood children making snowmen with accessories they have scrounged together—reading glasses, paperboy caps, cigars or pipes, and such things. They make me smile and help to remind me that the war hasn't taken every last drop of innocence. Not yet, anyhow. I will return to Cambridge soon, although it seems like a silly pursuit now with so much tragedy in the world. Please continue sending your letters here, as I will be sure to receive them from my parents. I am unable to send you my Cambridge address because I don't know which dorm building I will be assigned.

I think of you—where you sleep, what you are doing, who you see every day and who you talk to, what you think and dream about. I wait for your words.

I wish for happiness this year: an end to this war and our own suffering. I wish for you to come home.

The honesty of our thoughts and words are all we have to keep this frail garment of our relationship intact. We hardly know each other, and yet I also feel struck by a current of emotions for you that carry me through these obstacles. I can only imagine where you are, and you are right not to tell me, because my imagination is gruesome enough. I ask only that you do not write to me anything false, in moments of desperation or whatever fear may come to you. Please keep your head on your shoulders for both of us. I am not saying this to discourage you, only to safeguard my own heart while I am fighting my own silent war of not being near you.

I must also chide you for you thinking that the insanity of this war does not affect me—you seem to think I am having pleasant tea, buying pretty dresses, and laughing at common jokes when I know the realities of where you are and what could be happening to you. My girlfriend received a telegram last week regarding her fiancé, and I ran to console her. I won't tell you anymore, as I don't want those thoughts to spawn in your brain. I will be honest with you—I don't sleep at night, but I do try to imagine you in some special armour that will keep you safe. My imagination is strong,

for better or worse. I do keep your ring close to me. I do wait for you to be in my arms again.
   Be safe, love.
   Yours always,
   Ellie

He read her letter again and again. He had only received it the week before leaving his post in Normandy. She told him about the telegrams that had been delivered to the girls she knew and the boys who weren't coming home. There were dried tear marks on the paper. He wished she wouldn't write him about that business, but he understood. It was her way of telling him to be careful and to come home in one piece and breathing. He was having a hard enough time worrying about himself and the possibility of not seeing the next day through. He tried to maintain a single focus and a firm heart, although the reality struck him in the face daily. It amazed him that he was eventually able to reconcile the grim reality that a boy he had breakfast and coffee with in the morning might come back by nightfall with a sheet over him. It happened all too often. He worried about her twisting herself into a frenzy about his safety. He wanted to put her at ease and put his own mind at ease, as he lay on his bunk, away from the other men, and wrote to her.

March, 1945

Dear Ellie,
   I keep your photograph in my front pocket to protect my heart. I am convinced it will shield me from all bullets. You are my special armour; I am not teasing. You are my focus, my will to think and react as quickly and clearly as possible. You will only receive letters from me, and I pray no telegrams will come to you in the absence of my letters. I will not tell you the details of the conditions where I write these letters: we are moving around, and every post, every barrack is the same. The other men sometimes

keep themselves occupied with playing cards and looking at lewd photos of pinup girls. I think of you and put my pen to paper before I lose a thought or explode from a full heart. Some of the guys here have asked to see your photograph, but I tell them your face is sacred. I have only shown my close friend, Sam. He believes you are a glowing light, as do I.

There is talk of the war coming to an end, a small glimmer of light in the tunnel. I try to keep up my strength and move along and concentrate on following orders. I've made friends here, but I try not to make too many close attachments because I don't know what will happen to any of us. I've seen things that I will never talk about. I dream of you at night to take me away from here—even if it is for a brief while. It is good to have hope and I thank you for giving me your hope. Home sounds good: I lose touch with the idea of home at times. I am glad you are continuing your studies at Cambridge. I wouldn't want you to give up on your dreams. Remember, we have our futures to think about. In this place, there are days I can't see past the end of my nose, and other days all I can see is my whole life ahead of me. I look forward to your words, too. Let's stay strong, love.

Always,
Willis

Chapter 6

When Willis returned to London in May, he felt as though he were walking through a dream. His regiment had been instrumental in the liberation of Arnhem, and the end of the war had followed rapidly. The notion that the war was over and he had survived it all and come home almost unscathed had not yet sunk in. He doubted it ever would. Then he saw Ellie on the train platform wearing the same blue dress she had worn the day she saw him off to the unknown. It seemed strange how he was now returning to a different unknown. All of the men—for they had become men—were struck by the vast responsibility of starting a normal life. For some, their women were waiting for them, not knowing they weren't the same boys they knew from high school. Those boys were gone. The past was lost, and everything would be different.

Willis stepped off the train and into Ellie's arms and hard kisses. Her eyes were glistening, and her red mouth was stretched so wide he could see her molars.

"You're home, darling!" she exclaimed. "You're home!" He simply held her and said nothing. He couldn't speak, and he couldn't quite believe her words in his ear. *"You're home, the war is over, you're safe and you don't have to go back."* He held her tighter as she squealed and kissed his cheek. How would she ever understand the depth of what she was telling him? How could she ever know? They went to her waiting car.

"We must go see mother and father," she said.

"No, not yet," he replied. She stopped her hand from turning the ignition. "First, take me somewhere quiet for a while."

"Alright," she said softly and started the car. She took him to a nearby park, where they watched children and dogs run on the green grass.

"Thank you," he said. She took his hand in answer and sat quietly beside him. Once again, it was hard for him to believe that this innocent life had existed all along, not far away, while he had endured the blasts of gunfire and screams of dying men calling for their mommies. Still, he knew that wasn't fair; Londoners had endured their own personal struggles during the war years: the nighttime air raids, lost houses and family members, rationed foods, and the constant worry for their boys in uniform. He turned to her with an apologetic look.

"I didn't ask if you are okay," he said. "I know it hasn't been easy over here either. We heard about the recent V-weapon attacks from the Germans." She looked stunned.

"Of course I am okay. Yes, it's been horrible—we were lucky to make it through. There were many families who weren't so lucky. I don't want to talk about all of those horrible things; at least, not today. You're home and in one piece and that is all that matters to me now." She smiled at him. He smiled back.

"I mean, we haven't seen each other in so long, and so much has happened for both of us in that time. This must feel strange for you too," he said. "Are you okay?"

"Yes, I am now," she answered, and a tear escaped her long lashes. He put his arm around her and squeezed her shoulder hard, pinning him next to her. Willis wanted to ask her about their promise, but now wasn't the time. He noticed she was still wearing his promise on her left ring finger. He needed to look at the green grass for a while longer.

After breathing in the clean air for a while, they started to walk toward her parents' townhouse. Only hours before, Ellie had taken Willis' promise ring from her drawer and slipped it on. She felt optimistic, but she hadn't yet dared touch on the subject of their happily ever after. Ellie felt sad and awkward amidst her joy of having her love by her side again. She didn't know what she could have expected. She read the papers and listened to the radio broadcasts like everyone else. Still, she thought somehow he would come back to her clear and ready. She wasn't sure how fractured he was, and so she held his arm gently and said very little. It was true what he had said about the hardships on the home front. She had to shake it off somehow and focus on him. They were walking in a dream.

When they arrived at Ellie's home, her father opened the front door to greet them before they reached the landing.

"Hello, son," Mr. Birch extended a hand to him, and Willis took it firmly.

"Hello, sir."

"Good to have you home again," Mr. Birch said. He refrained from calling Willis "soldier," as the word seemed to leave a bad taste in everyone's mouths. They were proud of their soldiers and allies, and they had won the war, but at a great cost. At the beginning of the war, no one could have anticipated the number of years and men and women that would be lost. It was too much to bear, too many souls. Mr. Birch quietly led the couple into the house and gave his daughter a lingering look of tender sympathy as she passed him. Mrs. Birch was in a distant part of the house and came down to meet them a few moments later. She hugged Willis when she saw him, abandoning any formalities.

"Oh, thank goodness," she said softly. "You've been away far too long." Then she stood back to admire him in his uniform with a sad smile. Willis felt his shoulders relax as he looked from Mr. Birch to his wife. He still couldn't find words, and no one expected them. They ushered him into the next room, and Mr. Birch brought Willis a glass of brandy.

"I remembered," he said, handing Willis the glass.

"Thank you," Willis answered. He wondered why their servant wasn't tending to the drinks, but decided not to ask.

"We couldn't afford to keep Frederick," Mr. Birch said apologetically. It was clear that he wasn't apologizing to Willis, but to Frederick himself in his absence. "It really is a shame. He was part of our family. Oh, sure, our house is still standing, thank Christ, but nothing has been easy." Mrs. Birch silently took her husband's hand. Willis wasn't sure whether or not to feel sorry for them after seeing so many other families in far worse shape. Still, he understood how the war had touched the lives of everyone, and he bent his head down toward his glass, swishing it in his hand and sipping thoughtfully. Everything had changed so rapidly and unexpectedly in the recent months, leading up to the end of the fight. Ellie looked nervously from her parents to Willis. No one knew what to say next. Finally, her father continued, breaking the silence. "I know you have just returned, son, but do you think you might still pursue your dream of becoming a barrister?"

"I would still like to, yes," Willis looked up at him, "soon." He was eager to start his life again.

"That's good," Mr. Birch said. "You know, I thought about ringing my old colleague for you—the law professor at Cambridge. That is, if you don't mind. Let's see if we can get you enrolled in classes for the fall semester."

"I wouldn't mind that at all, sir," Willis answered. "I would be grateful."

"We are the ones who are grateful to you," Mr. Birch replied and then took a long sip of his own hard drink.

Willis wanted to turn the subject again, so he politely added, "And what a wonderful achievement for Ellie completing her art studies." Ellie beamed at Willis, and he gazed back at her with fresh eyes. Willis took another gulp from his glass and placed it on the small table beside him. Ellie's parents turned their attention to their daughter as well, who sat quietly across the room. She was like a tiny leaf shaking on a twig.

"Yes, we are very proud of everything she has done." Mr. Birch raised his glass to Ellie with open sincerity. Secretly, in his mind, he didn't fully understand or appreciate the importance of art in these times. He didn't believe, as Ellie did, that civilization was created on the foundation of art or that it would be the arts that would pull the people up from the rubble to recover from the damage of the past six years and rebuild and strengthen their spirits, cities, and cultures.

"You must see the beautiful piece Ellie painted for her master's project," Mrs. Birch chimed in.

"I would love to," Willis answered. "Mr. Birch, I also have something to ask you." Willis began feeling the effects of the brandy warm his chest and pleasantly flood his head.

"Oh?" Mr. Birch asked with a knowing look.

"Ellie, dear, come with me into the kitchen to put on some tea," Mrs. Birch said to her daughter hastily.

"Yes, of course, Mother," Ellie replied, blushing deeply. The two women then scurried out of the room, suppressing their smiles. The two men stood facing each other in the living room and then sat down again once the women had disappeared.

"I am eager to start my life," Willis began, "and I can't imagine starting my new life without Ellie. I would like your permission to ask her to marry me, sir."

"Good man!" Mr. Birch said simply and leaned forward to clink Willis' glass.

"I should tell you, sir, that I don't have a proper engagement ring yet. You must know that I gave her a promise ring before I left. My intentions are true."

"Just ask her, son. You don't need to wait for jewelry. Have you told your own parents yet?"

"Thank you, sir. No, I am going to send them a telegram tonight," Willis answered. "I hope they are pleased and not too disappointed about my plans to stay over here."

"I am sure your parents will be relieved to just know you are safe and in one piece," Mr. Birch said with a tone of parental authority. The women came back into the living room with a tray holding a large pot of tea, a small milk pitcher, a sugar dish, and cups and saucers. The men gave an appropriate sound of appreciation as Mrs. Birch played the role of *Mum* and poured the tea for all of them. Ellie watched Willis with a hopeful look, while her mother fussed over the tea and inquired about how many lumps of sugar. Willis caught Ellie's gaze and gave her a long, determined, and meaningful look. Then he winked at her, and she blushed all over again. When the evening began to die down, the family of three shuffled behind Willis to the front door, hugging him and shaking hands. Mr. Birch told him he would call his friend at the university in the next day or so and get the ball rolling. Ellie walked him outside and they stood together in the warm dusk. Willis took her hands in his and looked at her with strong intent.

"I don't have a proper engagement ring for you, Ellie," he started.

"I don't need another ring," she answered. "I have this one." He smiled at her romanticism.

"How would you like a gold band to sit beside your ring?" he asked. His eyes were cast down for a moment, and then he met her eyes, which had never moved from his face. Her eyes began to swell with small tears. She was shaking.

"More than anything," she said. "I would like that more than anything." He kissed her and held her as though she were the last thing that belonged to him. He watched her run back into the large house. He wasn't sure what he could give her at this time, except his words and bodily comfort, but he didn't want to wait any longer. He left her reluctantly and went with a noticeable lift in his step to find a hotel, trying to decide how to phrase the news to his parents in Canada. The next morning, he sent the following telegram:

DEAR MOM AND DAD:
I HAVE RETURNED TO ENGLAND SAFE. I
AM MARRYING ELLIE AND WILL REMAIN
LIVING HERE. WE WILL VISIT AT XMAS.

The message was terse, yet complete. Telegrams were expensive. Willis could imagine his mother clutching her heart. He had to live his own life. He had been away for too long to go back now. Somewhere, somehow, a cord had been cut.

Chapter 7

In early July, Willis stood opposite a fresh-faced young woman who wore a light lilac-coloured dress, which blended with the spectator flowers in the small garden. Sam stood next to him. The high sun beat down on their shoulders.

"Do you, Willis Hancocks, take Ellie Birch to be your lawful wedded wife, to have and to hold from this day forward, until deaths do you part?" The minister's voice floated into his conscience with gravity. Willis gulped.

"I do," he answered, quiet and solemn. He barely heard the same words being presented to the woman who would become his partner for eternity in only a few seconds.

"I do," she said. Next he was kissing her and a roar of clapping rose in his ears, and then, a moment later, they were being pulled apart by friends and family who were desperate to hug and kiss them as well. His parents weren't among the well-wishers. Ellie's parents had offered to pay for their trip, but they had regretfully declined with the excuse that they did not wish to travel so far away from home. Willis wasn't too surprised. Instead, his parents expressed their gratitude and passed along their joy and blessings, saying that they looked forward to seeing the new couple at Christmas. Willis wasn't sure if that was meant to ease the disappointment or to throw back his own words for making them wait so many months to see him. For the sake of the day, he chose to believe the former.

The rest of the summer afternoon moved along like a train: photographs; small, triangle-shaped sandwiches; drinks; toasts; dinner; and a three-tiered wedding cake with thick, white icing and bold ribbons. Willis sipped his champagne flute, half-listening to his friend Sam as he stared at the tiny couple on top of the cake. He wondered how long that tiny couple had existed, hand-in-hand and smiling. He was instantly embarrassed by the thought and returned his full attention to Sam who was talking about what on earth he wanted to do next.

"You got it all figured out pretty quick." He congratulated Willis with a soft, playful punch to the shoulder. Willis smiled.

"Why don't you attend school with me?" Willis proposed hopefully. "I'm starting courses at Cambridge in September. What are your interests?"

"I would have to dabble a bit, I think." Sam rubbed his chin. "Political Science, perhaps, or maybe some aspect of the field of business or law ... Cambridge, eh?" Willis knew he had his friend securely on the hook. They were both young, and they had futures to think about. He would talk to his new father-in-law about getting application papers for Sam as well.

"There you are, darling!" His wife burst into the conversation, raising a curious eyebrow at Sam. "You've been keeping him from me, have you?"

Sam laughed, "I wouldn't dream of it, but you know even married men still need their blokes."

"Note taken," she replied good-naturedly, "but not today. I need to steal him away for a bit if you'll excuse us, Sam." Sam stepped back and made a sweeping gesture of submission to the couple. Ellie dismissed him with equal grace, and Willis cocked his eyebrow at his friend while being dragged off by his wife. *His wife.* This was no longer quiet, young Ellie painting her imagination on canvases in her upstairs room. This was Ellie with real stars growing in her eyes and legal rights to him. Willis was promenaded around the garden to various circles of new faces, and later he was able to sit down at a small patio table, eat small, decorative sandwiches, and to reflect on the day and everything that lay ahead. To him the future looked like a prairie, an endless cycle of seasons. They would take everything one day at a time, one goal at a time, and focus on doing things right. In his mind, the simplicity of his goals and their life together pleased him.

When September came, Willis was supposed to be heading to Cambridge. All of the plans for his enrollment had been arranged. However, during the summer months and shortly after their wedding, he had taken a dire sharp turn as his cognitive mind began fighting with his emotional brain. Willis began waking up in the middle of the night in a cold sweat, screaming. Ellie was bewildered by his restless sleep and felt helpless. She would try to soothe his forehead, but he would swat her hand away and curse at her. Then he would hastily put on a jacket and wander the streets of their sleepy neighbourhood or sit in the backyard in his pajamas, sobbing. The faces of soldiers clouded his vision, fallen or scarred for eternity. He thought he had come back unscathed, like the sole survivor of a car wreck who is given the chance to simply stand up and walk away, but nothing was that easy. Night after night, he lived in the darkness of his mind, and in the daylight hours he dwelled behind thick walls of silence.

Ellie felt herself floating farther away from him, refusing to believe that it was the other way around. Fortunately, they had consummated their marriage, but they had experienced little intimacy since their first night together. She carried on and kept him organized and functional as best she could. She kept his routine: his favourite slippers in the morning, his newspaper waiting on the arm of his reading chair, his pants and shirts neatly pressed, and his meals prepared. She chattered to him endlessly about her impromptu visits with the other wives she met at the grocery store or something she had heard on the radio. Still, if she became too excitable or her words just became noise, he would quietly stand up, mutter an apology, and gravitate toward the bedroom to try and catch up on his sleep. She ignored his trance-like state and night terrors, and he ignored her altogether. On their one-month wedding anniversary, she decided to try to break through the unbearable silence and tension between them. He was sitting at the kitchen table, half-heartedly eating part of a sandwich, when she quietly took a bottle of aged wine out of the cupboard and popped the cork beside him. The cork hit the ceiling light and he jumped out of his chair and grabbed her, ready to throw her to the floor. His eyes were wild, and he began yelling, "For Chrissake, get down!" Then, when he recovered himself and saw that it was only a wine cork, he was immediately disoriented and embarrassed. He barked at her, "Goddammit, Ellie! What the hell are you doing?"

"I wanted to celebrate our first fucking month of marriage!" she yelled back at him. Tears were streaming down her cheeks. She was just as tired as him. He gave her a wounded look and walked out of the house.

He couldn't share his demons with her, and he didn't want to. She didn't deserve to know the horrors that lurked inside the dark corners of his memory. He felt useless as he began fading in and out of his own bodily awareness and blanking out in the one-way conversations Ellie tried to have with him. As the days went by, blurring together, he dreaded the night, and during the day he would glance at the four walls around him in every room and wish they weren't imprisoned there together. He had made everything happen too fast; there hadn't been time to get his feet back on solid ground. It wasn't her fault, of course, but he was beginning to feel himself slip downwards into a hole—following the fallen men into that mass grave swallowing all of them. He could almost feel the walls of his house crumbling around him, but the inner walls of his mind were crumbling instead.

By the end of the summer, Ellie had had enough. She had spent countless hours crying at her parents' house, while they tried to explain to her that she had never known the boy he was before the war. She'd met him in the heat of it all, when he was full of adrenalin and momentum. He had been thinking too much about his duty and survival to worry about much else. Boys died; you buried them and carried on. Now that the war was over, it was like hitting a brick wall. He had time now to remember.

In the same breath, Ellie's parents reminded her that she was his wife and needed to be strong to support him. "That is what wives do," they told her. "You are part of him now, and it's not just about you." They agreed with her that she wasn't equipped to care for him alone and assisted her in making arrangements to have him checked out by their family physician. It would be difficult to approach him with the suggestion, but the three of them managed to do it gingerly and with the right amount of sympathy. Ellie brought Willis to her parents' house one afternoon.

"Let's just stop in for tea, shall we?" she asked him. He knew the question was a rhetorical one, and that he didn't have the opportunity to say, "Let's not." So, instead, he followed her like a child. Willis hadn't stepped foot in his in-laws' house since they were first married, and now he seemed to enter the premises and move around cautiously, as though he had never been there before; new rooms, new walls. Mr. Birch cleared his throat, and Willis looked up at him expectantly.

"Willis, son," he began. "Ellie has told us that you are having ... um ... difficulty readjusting to life at home."

I'm not really home, Willis thought. At least, it didn't feel like the home he expected; but then, he didn't know what he had expected. He kept his lips tight.

"Perhaps you need some time on your own to sort things out?"

"Where?" Willis asked, astonished. His lips had become loose, despite his best efforts to not react.

"We're not sure. The best place to start might be a conversation. We have an excellent physician if you would like to sit down with him for a while? He is a veteran, you know. He might be able to shed some light on what you're experiencing," Mr. Birch rattled on hopefully. His wife touched his arm.

"I don't know," Willis said. "I suppose it couldn't hurt." He didn't look at Ellie. He couldn't bear to, but he felt her watching him with her strained, glistening eyes. He owed her this much. She had married someone broken.

Chapter 8

A week later, Ellie drove Willis to the physician's office. He trudged through the hall beside her, with her arm tucked into his. He wasn't sure if he was comforting her or if she was holding him up instead; they moved together as a unit, albeit awkwardly, as though in handcuffs. The door to the doctor's office was closed, and Ellie sprung forward nervously to open it for him and then stepped back to let him go in. This was his visit, not hers. He eyed her suspiciously for a moment and then went through the door. There was a small gathering of other people visiting the doctor just inside the entranceway, sitting in chairs and reading magazines. They all looked up at him: someone new.

"I'll be back in a moment, darling," Ellie chirped, and she left before he could even attempt to stop her. She shut the door soundly behind her and went outside to have a smoke. She didn't like doctors' offices. She didn't want anyone to be involved in their lives. She wished she could fix it by herself and that she was enough. She solemnly puffed on her cigarette, taking her time, and watched the small furl of smoke vanish into the breeze.

Inside the cramped waiting room, the minutes ticked by slowly. Willis looked around the room at the other patients, only just now taking them in. Strange, they were all young men who otherwise looked healthy as horses; but, perhaps, not so strange. So many of them had come back, haunted and broken; they continued to fight inner battles no one else could see. The men looked back at him with the recognition of suffering and then looked away. Ellie snuck back into the room. She opened the door and squeezed herself in as though she was disturbing a lecture or afraid to wake a room full of napping babies. She sat down next to him, picked up a magazine off the end table, and pretended to read it. Her eyes were blotchy; her gaze was fixed on the pages. Then she did something unexpected—she leaned on his arm. He reached over and placed his hand on her leg. It was the most intimate they had been in weeks. The door inside the waiting room opened, and the nurse poked her head out.

"Mr. Hancocks?" she called. He stood up.

"I'll be right here, darling," Ellie said. He nodded and followed the nurse through the door and down the white, narrow hallway.

"Please wait in here for a moment," she motioned to a little room on the right. "The doctor will be right with you." He muttered a thank you as she closed the door gently behind her. He looked at the certificate on the wall, the charts and instruments, and the cartoon pinups for the children. Inside himself, he felt like an old man who had accomplished nothing. The doctor came in; he was an older man, but he had a secret spark in him.

"Good day to you, sir," the old doctor said. He peered up from his chart to briefly look at Willis, and even in the brief moment, he seemed to be able to assess everything he needed to know. "What seems to be the trouble today?"

"It's not just today, Doc." Willis felt a barrier move up inside him. "I haven't felt right for a while. Nothing feels right."

"Nothing is a lot of something," the doctor replied quietly. "I think I know. I remember. I was there too."

"Mr. Birch mentioned you were a veteran," Willis said. He looked the doctor in the eye. "It's not good, is it?"

"No, it's not good, but it was necessary. People will remember for a long time. They might not know what we know, but they also won't forget."

"My wife doesn't know," Willis said. He had a lump in his throat. "I can't stop thinking about all those boys. We thought we became men ... maybe we did, but not in the right way. Why did I get to come back? Why am I so lucky? I should have stayed with those boys, you know?"

"There is a lot more you need to do. You've done it for crown and country, and now you have to do it for yourself. It's a different kind of battlefield, but you'll get through this one too." The doctor looked at him imploringly. "It's a textbook case of combat exhaustion. Will you let me help?" It was a common affliction that the doctor recognized all too well: the overwhelming stress and anxiety these soldiers experienced upon their reentry into family life after witnessing the horrors of war. Willis nodded his head slightly in response.

"Okay, then. I'm going to refer you to a psychiatrist I know, and he is a veteran as well. I'm guessing that he will probably recommend a place called Sunny Acres. I think you just need a chance to catch your breath. You're not alone, you know; not by a long shot. We'll get you back in the saddle, son.

When Willis came out of the doctor's office, Ellie clutched her purse and stood up.

"Where do we go now?" she asked her husband.

"Home," he replied. She looked agitated.

"Hang on, dear. I'll come in a second," she said as she gently persuaded him into the hallway. The doctor was still lingering in his little doorway. She approached him with purpose. "Doctor, can I have a word with you?"

53

"Of course. Come step inside for a moment." He motioned her into his space. She nodded curtly and went into the narrow hallway, and he closed the door behind them.

"What do you mean sending him home? He's obviously disturbed. Can't you put him somewhere for a little while?"

"I've referred him to a psychiatrist to sort out his ... problems. For now, he just needs some rest. He's endured a long haul."

"Well, what am I supposed to do with him?" Ellie asked. She was nervous.

"Why don't you try being his wife," the doctor answered. She bristled visibly, trying to hold back angry, tired tears and turned on her heel to leave.

That night Ellie seemed to fall asleep with no problem, but Willis lay awake on his pillow, partly keeping the nightmares at bay and also trying to absorb everything the physician had said to him. Eventually, he rose from his sheets and headed to the kitchen. He wasn't hungry, but he was lonely. He picked up the phone and dialed the operator for Sam's house.

"Hello?" a voice on the other end answered groggily.

"Hello, Sam," Willis croaked. "I'm sorry to wake you. I wasn't sure who to call."

"What time is it?"

"I don't know. It's long after midnight," Willis answered.

"Are you okay?"

"I'm not sure. Can we meet?"

"Sure, come on over," Sam replied. He was renting a house in Surrey. Willis swiftly got dressed and headed out to the Tube without so much as leaving a note for his wife. When he finally reached Sam's residence, Sam had the beers chilling in the fridge and welcomed him in with a firm handshake and a one-armed embrace. They sat at his kitchen table in the stark light.

"I don't know what is happening," Willis began. "I think I'm starting to lose it. Everything seems to be crumbling."

"I get it," Sam said. His lips were pursed.

"Is it the same for you?"

"I get the night sweats and the recording in my mind won't let up," Sam confessed. "All those boys we knew. Everything we saw."

"Only you don't have to hide it or explain it to anyone. I can't talk to Ellie about everything I saw and what I had to do. I don't want her to have the burden. She can imagine enough of it already."

"Which do you think is worse? Having someone by your side trying to help you, who can't begin to know how? Or having no one there at all?"

"I'm here," Willis said.

"Yeah, I know, but you're just as fucked up by it all as I am." They sat in silence for a minute and then broke out in sad, hysterical laughter.

"Yeah, I guess I can't help much," Willis said. "Jesus. I want to know why we were we so lucky to come back. What makes us so special? There was so much waste. What do we have to offer?"

"Beats the crap out of me." Sam shrugged. "I don't think we should read too much into it … It was all a crap shoot, wasn't it? Who was more alert? Who was the better soldier? Whose number, well, just came up?"

"At least we can talk. Not everyone who came back wants to talk, and everybody else just doesn't understand. We went to war, we won the war, and now we're back home in one broken piece and everyone expects us to forget about it and move on with the world. We know what really happened and what we had to do to get through the whole damn thing," Willis said quietly.

"I've got your back, mate," Sam said and tapped his friend's beer can.

"Thanks, Sam," Willis said. He grew quiet again and took another swig of his beer.

"Poor Ellie, though," Sam mused. "It must be hell for her."

"I am thankful she doesn't understand."

"I get it. Still, it doesn't make for much of a marriage when you can't tell your partner about the secrets in your heart."

"Yes, well ... speaking of secrets, she also doesn't know I'm here. I should get back and slip into bed before morning."

"Stay in touch, Willis, and take care of yourself." Sam stood up from his chair to see his friend out. "What happens next?"

"I saw a physician today; Ellie wanted me to go. He said I am suffering from combat exhaustion and stress."

"Makes perfect sense."

"He referred me to a psychiatrist for further observation. I might be going away for a while, just to gain some peace and perspective."

"You do whatever you think is best to get back on your feet, solider."

"Soldier," Willis repeated. There was an air of reminiscence in his voice, a longing and sadness as he was thinking about a remnant of another time and world. He tipped his paperboy cap and left his friend.

A week later he was in another waiting room at the psychiatrist's office. Ellie dutifully sat beside him, looking prim and grim. When he was finally ushered in to meet with the doctor, the procedure was similar: a smaller, isolating room with distractive photos on the stark-white walls. The psychiatrist breezed through the door after one knock and lowered his glasses slightly on his nose to look at him.

"Ah, Mr. Hancocks. Yes, I see here that you've seen my dear colleague, and he has kindly referred you to me to have a chat," he started with ease.

"Yes, he thought you might be the best person to talk to," Willis answered. He felt agitated. The doctor chuckled.

"Well, I don't know about being the best, but I'm certainly qualified." He smiled and gestured vaguely to a certificate on the opposing wall. The conversation went smoothly, and the psychiatrist simply confirmed what the doctor had already guessed: combat exhaustion and anxiety.

"There's no shame in taking it a bit slower; turning life down a notch or two, if you will." The psychiatrist smiled again. He looked at Willis as though he was a child, but there was a large degree of empathy as well. Willis mentioned that the doctor said he was a veteran of WWI. The older man looked thoughtful and stuck his chest out a little more as he recalled the Great War. He said it with bravado, which irked Willis slightly, only because it sounded like *his* war somehow trumped the war he had just fought. Then, he realized, each man had his own attachment and claim to victory days. Every war, and each man's part in it, was something to wear on his sleeve every day, but at the same time, to speak of seldom and hold down deep; it was a privilege and a burden kept only between all who had suffered it. No one else could understand. The men momentarily looked at each other with an equalizing gaze.

"I think some time spent at Sunny Acres would do you a world of good. There is much more in store for you in this life, young man; you need to have the space, time, and rest to pull your pieces back together and prepare yourself to face whatever is behind the next corner. Please do take my advice," the psychiatrist said, handing him a letter of referral. Then he rose and opened the door. "Carry on."

Two weeks later Ellie had helped him pack his bags and drove up to Sunny Acres in the countryside. Their home life was unbearable; an invisible fault line or barbed wire fence existed in the middle of their bed. She wanted to touch him but didn't know how. She also didn't know the same thoughts lurked in his mind. A deep, sad chasm lay between them. They both emerged from the car just inside the gates and took in the grounds. There were young men in matching pajamas and housecoats roaming around alone or chatting casually with an attendant or companion, and a few more reading quietly on the scattered park benches or contemplating the clouds and flowers. The world seemed to slow down already. Willis was drawn to the place, but also skeptical of this strange environment.

Chapter 9

Willis voluntarily resigned himself to be admitted into the veteran's hospital's care. Ellie stood by him as he signed on the dotted line then demurely kissed him goodbye and promised to visit on the weekends. She wanted him to have as much space and rest as possible and felt a sharp pang that she was somehow partly to blame for his anxiety. As she was leaving, she watched the pretty, young nurse touch his elbow and lead him to his dorm. She was envious of anyone who could get that close to him. Their last intimate interaction had been weeks before in the doctor's office. She savoured the lingering sensation of his body's warmth, however brief. She walked out to the car, rattled the key in the door, and then sank into the driver's seat, gripping the steering wheel and breathing in the solitude; she exhaled slowly. She wasn't sure about this freedom, this abandonment, or this separation from what should be her life.

WILLIS

It took Willis a while to adjust to daily life at Sunny Acres. He knew that he was surrounded by people who could relate to his state of being, but he was reluctant to make any new connections. They all seemed to be content to stay in their fabricated, well-insulated, haunted bubbles. He was also disoriented by the notion of working to relax. A fragment of him still anticipated random bunk bed inspections. He couldn't accept that there weren't any strings and that he was not being institutionalized, kept away as punishment for being mentally unstable. He couldn't accept that he was given a legitimate opportunity to find his footing, to breathe and refocus. For reassurance, he attached himself to the person closest to him, the person in his line of sight. The nurse who was assigned to him was attractive and sweet, and he decided she was safe. Although he had the opportunity to connect with the other men, he didn't want to relive those stories they were all afraid to tell, and he sensed that they didn't want their bubbles punctured either. They were all there to get away from the reasons why they were there.

One morning, after a few days of settling in, he saw his nurse breeze through the communal area.

"Good morning," he said. She stopped in her white shoes. She looked startled, diverted from her daily routine of checking on the residents. Her face instantly warmed and an easy smile graced her lips. She was a distance away, but he could see that she was not being phony.

"Good morning, Willis." She nodded. She took one step toward him, but she wasn't committing herself.

"I never did ask you, what is your name?"

"I did tell you when you were admitted, but I think you were a bit dazed. You were still taking it all in. My name is Daisy—and if you say the word *duck*, I'll wallop you." She gave him a levelling gaze, and he couldn't help chuckling.

"Daisy," he repeated. "I was thinking more of a delicate flower."

"Thank you, Willis," she answered. Her guard was down, and she seemed to retract her mock hostility. It was a reflex from years of teasing. She bent one leg behind the other shyly. She seemed to be somebody who was uncomplicated, and that was what he needed. During his first couple of weeks at the sanctuary, the pair took regular strolls together on the grounds. He slyly pulled out his pack of cigarettes and poked one between his dry lips and lit it as she told him that she had recently graduated from nursing school. He told her very little about himself. He liked listening to her: how she loved to read books and sometimes make up her own stories about people, how she had four younger siblings and helped raise them because her mother was on her own and worked all the time, how she grew up taking care of people and knew she wanted to help people for the rest of her life. He told her she had a kind, open heart, and that was a rare gift. One afternoon, as they walked casually around the hospital, she stopped and looked at him. He tapped his cigarette ash on the ground.

"I'm really not supposed to spend so much time with you, you know," she said decidedly. "I'm not supposed to fraternize with patients."

"We're not fraternizing." He smirked. "I haven't even tried to hold your hand. We're just being friendly. You're my nurse. You're supposed to be friendly, aren't you?"

She looked unconvinced and gave a small "humph." She wanted to say "you're married," but she was wary of insinuating anything. She liked him, and she felt the feeling was mutual. He was handsome, and his wife seemed like a cold fish; at least, she'd gathered that much from what she saw of her behavior around him. His wife didn't seem comfortable in her own skin, and his posture was clearly moving away from her. Daisy wished she was somewhere different with Willis and that they were different people in another situation.

The next weekend, when Ellie dutifully came to visit her husband, she found him with his nurse in the main room. Only a few other patients were milling about and his nurse was leaning over Willis while he sat at a table; she had a strange smile on her face and tittered at something witty he'd said. He was drawn into her, lost in some secret conversation. She stopped in the doorway and watched them quietly until his nurse looked up, and her seductive smile vanished as she stepped back from the table and muttered something about needing to check on someone. Ellie's gaze turned on Willis, dismissing the young girl in a heartbeat. Willis returned her steady gaze but with much less hostility. He looked calm and indifferent.

"Ellie, love, is it Saturday already?" he said. "I was just getting my daily vitamin."

"I can see that," Ellie responded. "Yes, Willis, it is Saturday. I suppose your days go by in a different rhythm from the rest of the world." She kept her voice steady and calm as well. This was a charade, a play they were both forced to be in and deliver their well-scripted lines. He gently pushed out an opposing chair for her with his foot. Ellie accepted the offer. She had so many questions resting on her tongue: *Isn't she a bit young for you? Aren't you supposed to be resting? Don't you miss me at all? What the hell do you think you're doing? Why can't we be that way with each other again? Where did you go?* The questions kept coming, falling on top of each other. She still managed to swallow each one down into the lining of her stomach. It was her own silent victory, but she didn't feel like she had won anything.

They kept the conversation light: he asked about her parents and if she was taking care of herself. He was resentful of the fact that her parents were the ones supporting her, emotionally and financially; it wasn't their job anymore, but he wasn't equipped. He could feel all of their disappointment in him; he was certain of it, the conversations that went on about him—without him. It made him feel inferior and useless. Deep down, he was sulking like a child, but he tried to put on a weak front and keep up his guard. It was the most he could do to be in control. He didn't ask about her painting or social life, and she didn't ask about anything except if he was sleeping better.

"Yes," he answered. "Most nights have been pretty good."

"I'm glad," she said. She was being sincere. *I'm glad you're here. I'm glad they are taking care of you. I wish I could.* There were so many unsaid thoughts that she was afraid to confide in him: afraid her desires and concerns would cause him more stress. She didn't see how opening up to him could begin to mend them. "I'm sorry, Willis. I do have another appointment to rush off to."

"That's alright, Ellie," he said softly. "I'll see you next Saturday, then? I'll mark off the days this time." She nodded and reluctantly left. He knew there was no appointment. There was simply nothing left to say.

When Ellie arrived at home, she stood in the hallway and drummed her fingers beside the telephone. Then she hastily picked it up and dialed the operator for Sunny Acres. She reached the administration office and asked to speak with the head nurse. She tried to sound as unassuming as possible as she expressed her concern that one of their nurses had seemed to be interacting inappropriately with her husband, who was recently admitted as a resident patient. The head nurse assured her that she would look into the matter and thanked her for her phone call. She added, in a stiff voice, that she apologized for any upset this matter may have caused and that management would not tolerate any sort of "hanky-panky." Ellie thanked the head nurse and apologized on her end for potentially creating any hassle.

The following day, Daisy was brought into the administration office, lightly reprimanded, and given transfer papers to sign confirming that she would work at another hospital in the neighbouring county. She left the office holding back indignant tears, trying to absorb their explanation for her dismissal: she was too friendly with the patients and treading on a dangerous line that shouldn't be crossed. She was told that she was young and new to the profession; she wouldn't have a black mark on her record, but she should watch herself. This kind of behavior was not acceptable.

"I see. We're just treating them like inmates, right?" she scoffed as she walked out the door.

Chapter 10

The next day, Willis looked around for Daisy and couldn't find her anywhere.

Finally, he relented and asked a fellow resident if he had seen her. The other veteran asked him if it was the little brunette, and when he answered "yes," the man shook his head with a grin.

"She was a pretty one," he said regretfully. "Too bad she had a 'thing' for one of the patients—I'm thinking now it was maybe you who signed her walking papers."

"What?"

"Yeah, I saw her march out of here with her luggage, accompanied by the management this morning," he said. "She looked pretty fierce. Real shame, that is." Willis bent his head but recovered surprisingly quickly.

"Ah well, she was nice to talk to for a while," he sniffed. "She helped me get settled in this place."

"We all needed a hand with that—it's not easy, is it? They bring us home in pieces and then expect us to be glued back together somehow. The word 'relax' isn't in my vocabulary anymore. I feel more like I'm hiding, really."

"Yeah, I'm the same way," Willis said.

"I'm Brett." The other man reached his hand out. Willis took it gratefully and introduced himself as well. "It's hard to make friends here too. No one wants to talk about themselves, even though we all know."

"You seem to know a lot about this place. How long have you been here?" Willis asked. He didn't want to admit that this man had seemed to read his thoughts, but then he figured it wasn't much of a secret.

"A couple of months," Brett said. He tossed his half-smoked cigarette into the landscaped flower bed. "You just got here, didn't you?"

"A few weeks ago," Willis answered. The other man nodded again, knowingly.

"What regiment and rank?"

"First Canadian Army. Private. You?"

"Royal British Army. Sniper. Enough said." He smiled grimly. "Yeah, it takes a while to get used to this place." Then Brett patted Willis on the shoulder and carried on down the garden stone path on his own.

Willis wasn't sure why, but he felt a sudden rapport with Brett, although the other veteran didn't seem to want to pry, he did appear to be open. Willis needed a friend—he didn't need to hash everything out, but he did need to feel a healing connection if he was going to make use of being in this place. It seemed ridiculous to just sit alone and wallow in the dark. Brett also appeared to be receptive to being "sought out." The two bonded quickly. Over the passing weeks, their conversations moved away from trivial subjects—hobbies, sports—and gradually came closer to the bone.

"So, married, right?" Brett lifted an eyebrow at his new friend.

"Yeah, does it show?"

"Well, you have that shackled, twitchy, married look about you." Brett smiled. "I'm attached to the old ball and chain too."

"Happy?" Willis asked. He wasn't sure what he hoped his answer would be. Did he want to find company with someone who wasn't sure about where his life was going? Or did he want to have some hope that people could be mended and carry on after the fracture of war? He didn't want to believe that they were all being thrust back into the arms of strangers.

"I was happy," Brett mused. "I still love her."

"That's a start," Willis said. His friend looked at him sideways.

"What about you?" Brett asked pointedly. Willis squirmed.

"I met my wife during the war, while I was on leave in London. I made a weak promise to her—maybe it was just a promise to keep me going and help me to survive. I guess I was infatuated with her. I don't know if it was real love, and I'm not sure what it is now. I married her as soon as I could after the war. I wanted to get on with it and start living a normal life. I guess I was just happy to be alive and eager to move ahead. That's why I'm here, I suppose. I reached a breaking point, because I didn't give myself a chance to get the tread back on my shoes."

"Well, we were high school sweethearts. She wanted to get hitched before I was shipped off. I knew I wanted to marry her, but I'm not sure I was ready to take the plunge that young. Honestly, I just wanted to make it legal so that I could get into her panties. I was afraid I might never get the chance again."

"Any kids?"

"No, thank Christ." He gave a sad chuckle. "I'd make a horrible father. I need to figure myself out before I can even think about taking care of anyone else. I don't even know what I can give to her anymore. She married a boy. I'm not sure who came back to her, and she doesn't know either. I don't think she'll ever know." He was quiet for a long time, and then he said, "They were kids, you know. Christ, we killed kids." They hadn't talked much about their experiences in the war, and Willis wasn't sure he could go there. He knew he needed to, if only to help his friend; he needed to reach back into the dark place—this was a way to acknowledge the pain and confusion, the aftermath. He didn't know where they were supposed to go from there.

"We were just kids too," Willis said. "We were all kids—hormonal idiots with guns. We can't be blamed for that."

"I don't know. I don't think I can justify any of it," Brett replied. "Anyhow, I think I might be going home soon." He absentmindedly began toying with a small, silver cross that hung around his neck.

"That'll be good," Willis replied.

"Yeah, it may be good for everybody." Willis dismissed this offhand comment, but it rattled something dark in the back of his mind. He decided to keep a closer eye on his friend. However, Brett started to spend more time in his dorm, and Willis rarely saw him as the ensuing week went by.

One morning he heard a woman's shrill scream while he was playing solitaire and then witnessed a commotion in the hall near the nurses' station. The nurses and a few men in white clothing were running down the hall toward the woman's screams. Willis sat frozen at the table in the communal room with a card wavering in his hand; he couldn't see what was happening. He could hear gasps and muttering, and then the same men jogged past him, less urgently. They returned a few minutes later with a cot on wheels. Willis had noticed the ambulance parked outside in the adjacent lot. It was a hospital of sorts, after all; but the thought of an ambulance being there never concerned him. It was simply protocol, a safety measurement. Now, in this confused moment, it was critical. A man was wheeled out of the building with a sheet draped over his face. Willis felt his blood run cold. *Brett*, he thought and tried to finish his solitaire game. Eventually, one of the nurses came into the room. She stopped when she saw Willis, and her chest gave a small heave as she approached him. She sat down beside him quietly and watched him place his last card on the end row.

"I came out on top that time," he said.

"Willis," she began, "I'm so sorry to tell you this, Willis. Brett is dead."

"I know," Willis answered in a steady voice. "How did he end it?" He wanted to endure this by processing it as another casualty of war, but his mounting emotions wouldn't let him; it was a switch he could usually flip on, but not this time.

"By asphyxiation ... he used his bed sheet," the nurse replied grimly. "You two seemed to be friends."

"The last time we chatted was about a week ago. He said he was getting ready to go home," Willis said. "I should have known what he meant. None of us can really go home after where we've been."

"I'm not sure you could have changed his mind. He confided a few things to me, but I didn't know he was set on getting out," she said sadly. "I did know that he struggled with the memory of all the things he had done."

"He was a soldier following orders and fighting for his country. He should have been decorated when he returned home—not swept under the carpet." Willis grimaced. "We all had a dirty job to do, and we had another duty to our families to try and not get ourselves killed while doing it." Every one of them had broken their moral compass along the way.

"I guess his remorse was too great to bear; he wanted atonement," she replied.

"Excuse me," Willis stood up and left the room. He walked back to his dorm in a daze, sat on his bed, and shed his first angry tears—for all those who had been lost and those who were still lost, including him.

Willis decided it was time to leave Sunny Acres and carry on in the real world. The veteran's hospital was not a place to be cured; it was simply a place to keep the troubled men out of sight for a while—a place that only created more isolation and the opportunity for time to think. He had been kept away in there for three months, and in the weeks that passed, he wasn't interested in reading a book, painting a picture of the garden flowers, or watching the clouds turn into animals—essentially letting his mind churn into butter. A phone call was made and his release papers were signed.

The drive home was tense as Ellie kept her eyes on the road and a firm grip on the wheel. Willis watched the world go by outside his window. She felt as though she had picked up a hitchhiker and was anxious to get him to his destination or, at the very least, drop off point as quickly as possible. She didn't want to bring him home. That night, after a silent dinner, she got ready for bed and waited nervously for him to slide under the cover. They lay in the dark for a long time, neither one of them finding sleep. Suddenly, he rolled over next to her body and, in a primal fashion, began fondling her breasts. Ellie took in a sharp breath and then gradually relaxed. He found her mouth, and his tentative tongue began exploring its dark cave of unsaid things. They smothered each other's excuses and apologies, their hollow words. Now was not the time for chatter.

 He wasn't sure if he actually missed her or craved her, or if he just needed to thrust himself onto another living human being for warmth and to remember that he was alive too.

 She didn't resist him, and he didn't try to guess at what she was thinking. It didn't matter. This was simply about flesh and being alive. Ellie moaned under his urgent fingers, as they caressed and molded, and finally entered her. Then he unceremoniously hoisted himself on top of her and took her with urgency. He was quick and then collapsed on her with heavy breath. She held him a long time in her arms, still not speaking. Eventually, he rolled back off her and fell asleep facing the opposite wall. She did the same and clutched her pillow; the white flag was down and they were back on enemy lines.

Chapter 11

The next morning, Willis woke up before Ellie. He crept out of the bedroom and went downstairs. He recalled the night before in a dreamy state, but instead of feeling rekindled, he felt more empty and alone. It wasn't right. He opened the front door and found a rolled-up newspaper on the step. He took in the street view—green and peaceful with leafy trees and landscaped gardens. Beyond their quiet street, there was chaos—rubble, death, tears—he was sure of it. The world hadn't been glued back together so quickly. He carried the paper to the kitchen table, opened the fridge, and pulled out a beer. As he pulled back the tab, Ellie came into the room and began making coffee. She peered over at him as he read the front page and slugged back his beer. She sat across from him, sipping her coffee and waiting to read the daily news. They didn't discuss the night before; instead, they went back into their safe bubbles. There was no normal in their house. Neither one of them was heading out the door to embrace the world. Ellie would get dressed and retreat to her painting studio in the attic, and Willis would put on his clothes and jump start his day. There were a couple of fix-up jobs around the house that he wanted to tackle. Unfortunately, two more beers delayed him and then he felt compelled to take a nap on the couch. A few hours later, Ellie found him, rolled her eyes, and stepped out to drive to the grocer.

When she returned, Willis was still asleep on the couch. There was another open beer can on the coffee table. She put away the groceries and hesitated for a moment about deciding whether or not to prep for dinner. She toyed with the keys in her hand. It seemed that she would probably be eating by herself anyhow, so she picked up her keys and stepped back out. However, instead of hopping back in the car, she opted to ride the train to Victoria Station. The fresh air and exercise would maybe help gunge out the dark cobwebs that were forming in her mind. Ellie began taking notice of the people around her. Where were they going? Were they heading somewhere with a purpose or merely filling in the day, chasing something or escaping from the walls of their own homes? She felt alone in the crowd, but she was sure she couldn't be alone. She told herself that everyone else was also putting on their nice clothes and a shielding smile to get through the day: they all had made sacrifices of some kind.

When Ellie reached Victoria Station, she pointed her feet in the direction of the National Gallery. It was a place she visited often for inspiration, motivation, and comfort. It was a place she understood, and yet it still posed challenging questions about the artists and their work. How did they find the time, inspiration, and courage to break through the barriers of their time, rise above the politics and social expectations to find a quiet space in their head—a sliver in their life—and create art? She knew she was fortunate to have the physical space and time to work on her paintings—not to mention her parents' financial support—but now it felt like a frivolous, indulgent pursuit rather than a life's calling. Still, it was her anchor—her canvas was a vessel to purge all the black out of her heart. Similarly, looking at the works of noted artists and dissecting their perceptions of art and technique helped bring a sense of order to her world; it was a distraction from the chaos of the outside world, at least the world she knew—albeit a new chaos, but this inner world was more contained and measured somehow. For a long time she sat undisturbed in a small exhibition room featuring Van Gogh, gazing at the world through his eyes. The feature exhibit was Van Gogh's *Sunflowers*, and she was most drawn to the painting *Two Cut Sunflowers* (1887). The painting was slightly more obscure. The most recognizable painting of his Sunflowers period was the one that contained the wilting sunflowers in a vase. This painting focused on two sunflower heads, seemingly embracing each other, with all of their light contrasted against a dark blue background. Although the edges of the flowers were curled in, there was a striking sense of the sunflowers, the center focus of the painting, overpowering the blue gloominess that surrounded them.

Somewhere, outside the focus scope of her mind, she sensed footsteps entering the room. It was the middle of the week and near closing time; she had the luxury of being free to roam around the city when most women were either cleaning up dinner plates or bathing babies. The footsteps stopped beside the bench, and she turned to find a man standing there. He had an odd smile on his face.

"Miss Birch, I thought that was you." He grinned. She searched his face for a moment; then a light shone through her eyes, as though someone had pulled a switch, and her lips spread to show a wide, toothy smile.

"Why, Mr. Hendrell," she beamed, "what an unexpected surprise!" He silently motioned to the bench with a question on his face. "Oh, yes, please do sit down," she replied. She felt a sudden heart flutter. Mr. Hendrell was one of her art instructors at Cambridge. He was in his thirties—fairly young to hold his prestigious position at the college, but he had earned it. He had a master's degree in art history and was an accomplished artist in his own right. He began teaching at Cambridge prior to the war, and the school had been able to maintain him throughout the war years, protecting him against the draft and holding firm that he was as an irreplaceable asset to their institution and future students. They were fortunate to have him, and she had felt privileged to be in his class. He was Ellie's first academic crush. He had taught art history, theory, and technique, but also invited a freestyle mode of learning, where he encouraged the students to bring their own works into the classroom for constructive critique. He was a bit bohemian—not stuffy like some of the other instructors, who believed the great artists of the world had already passed and there was no room or possibility to surpass the greats. Those instructors felt they were teaching appreciation, not growing a new crop of painters who could copy or reinvent what had already been mastered.

"How are you, Miss Birch?" he continued. It was custom in the classroom to address each other by last names, and it was a hard habit to break.

"I'm fine, I suppose," she answered honestly. "But I must tell you my name isn't Birch anymore. I'm married now."

"Ah, I see. I shouldn't be surprised," he said. "So, what do I have the pleasure of calling you now?"

"Well, since we are no longer in a teacher-student relationship, why don't you call me Ellie?" She smiled. Mr. Hendrell smiled back broadly.

"Peter," he said, holding out his hand. She shook it firmly.

"Wonderful to see you, Peter," she said.

"Likewise," he said. "I would ask you if you'd like to go and get a coffee with me, but I'm guessing you should be at home."

"I probably should," she answered. "The offer is tempting, though. Will you be here Saturday? I have shopping plans."

"Saturday then," he confirmed. They agreed to meet at the gallery, in the entrance lobby. For the next few days, Ellie was on edge; Willis never noticed. He was too busy getting drunk and popping pain medication for his headaches and sleepless nights. When

Saturday finally came, Willis was already gone in the morning, gone to visit Sam she expected. She took the train into London and walked hurriedly to the art gallery. She waited in the crowded lobby, watching the people mill about before getting in line to pay admission to see the exhibits. A finger lightly tapped her on the shoulder and she whirled around. Peter stood there looking at her with the same confident smile.

"Shall we?" he asked. She took his arm and they left the art gallery. As they walked down the front steps, Peter said "I know a great little coffee place. *The Daily Grind*—isn't that clever? They serve a really nice blend." He was taking the lead, and she liked it. He felt so comfortable. She knew it was dangerous, but she told herself that she needed this—she was lonely; she needed someone to meet her on common ground, to share ideas and just talk and smile.

They began meeting every Saturday, and the arrangement was always the same: meet in the bustle of the art gallery first and then escape to an intimate place to chat. They peered at each other over the rims of their coffee mugs, sipping, smiling, and enjoying their conversations. She gradually confided in him about her engagement to Willis during the last year of the war and then their rushed marriage when he returned. She told him about his trouble readjusting to civilian life. Her tone was laced with bitterness, but there was sorrow and sympathy there as well. She was tired and frustrated, but also sad and somewhat guilty about her inability to heal her husband, to bring him back. Peter listened with a compassionate ear, but he also tried to veer her away from the topic of her husband and help her focus on her own ambitions. He asked her if she was still painting.

"Yes," she said. "My art keeps me going most days."

"That's good," he said. "I always thought you had a great talent."

"Oh, come on," she laughed. "I only brought in one or two pieces, and my technique, or lack of it, was torn to shreds by the other students."

"I could see what they couldn't yet—a unique quality. Perhaps they were a little envious that you were trying to do something different, and they still didn't know how to break away from the paint by numbers." He shrugged. "I would love to see what you are working on now."

She put down her coffee cup and toyed with the handle. The idea was new and tempting. She hadn't been working in any serious fashion; mostly, her paintings were borne of venting, but didn't great art stem from raw emotion? She wondered how he would perceive her work: all the dark colours with only hints of light. No one else had seen her work. Would he think she was mad? Would he approve?

"I will bring a small canvas next week," she relented.

"Excellent." He smiled.

The next week, she carefully covered a smaller, more portable canvas and headed out to meet Peter. She hadn't seen Willis since the evening before. He had taken to coming home from Sam's place with cheap whisky on his breath. He would sometimes come into their bedroom and lean over her—checking on her—as she pretended to sleep and then lumber back downstairs to sleep on the couch. Most mornings he was either still passed out or nowhere to be found. The morning she smuggled out her painting was of the latter.

She revealed the painting to Peter at their usual coffee shop. He held it at arm's length away from him, scrutinizing. There were deep purples, blues, and dark greys intertwined in the center and overlapping slightly in the corners, as though a great dark bomb had gone off in the painting. In the very center there was a ball of orange, yellow, and red, like a heart beating, and all the darker colours came bursting out of it—bleeding, dripping off the edge of the canvas in small, fragmented rays. It was clear that a dark exterior surrounded and threatened this ball of light and joy, or perhaps it was the light and joy that was striving to overcome and push out all the gloom. The painting had the impression of going in two directions; it was alive and moving—reaching out and pulling in.

"You have a gift, Ellie," Peter said. "This is a painting of your heart and everything happening to your heart." Ellie sucked in her breath and felt tears resting on her mascara lashes, trying to escape. She blotted them away and gave him a validating look. She simply held the moment deep within her, conscious of the fear that if she tried to say something she would say much more than was necessary. Peter continued talking instead. "I am organizing an art exhibit in the summer at a venue downtown. I would love to share my gallery space with you." It was the opportunity of a lifetime, and she eagerly jumped at the chance.

"Oh, yes, I would love that too," she gushed. After they finished their coffee, he escorted her back to the train station as usual. He squeezed her hand before she left; a small, affectionate gesture, which now held a deeper layer of meaning: a promise, a bond, a nonverbal agreement. She squeezed his hand in response and boarded the train with her painting tucked under her arm.

They carried on their secret rendezvous for the next six months, always meeting at the art gallery and then making their way to The Daily Grind; it became a hideaway, a portal to another existence where they could be together and dwell in their world of art and abstraction. Peter's art exhibit was in June, and they were in a flurry of plans and heightened excitement. She knew she was living a double life, but she told herself that she deserved this—this escape from the misery of her plagued husband and the chance to revel in her creative outlet, her passion, and the possibility to make it grow into more than a hobby, a quiet interest kept in the attic under sheets. She also found Peter to be a kindred connection to that world she longed to be in.

One Saturday when she returned home, Willis was sitting at the kitchen table. He looked surprisingly sober. Ellie and Peter had been surveying the gallery space where they would be showing their joint exhibit in a month's time. Somehow, Ellie had managed to keep the whole event under wraps, although it wasn't difficult to keep Willis away from her other life. He never seemed interested in anything she did. She had taken the same painting that she'd first shown Peter, because he thought it should be her feature piece, and she wanted to see where it would hang in the gallery and how it would look.

"Where were you all afternoon?" Willis asked. Then he noticed the covered painting under her arm, "And what is that?"

"It's a painting of mine," she answered in an even tone. She opted to ignore his first question.

"For whom?" He squinted at her.

"What do you mean, *for whom*?" she shot back. "I showed a friend I met for coffee. I ran into an old classmate of mine a while back." If her story was closer to the truth, she wouldn't have to worry about hiding a tremor in her voice. "We were simply comparing notes and catching up," she retorted. She didn't dare tell him that she had been meeting this friend once a week for months.

Her tone was flippant, and he didn't like it. Still, he had no reason to mistrust her. He couldn't expect her to stay in the house all day.

"Fine," he said. "Can I see it?" She froze in the hallway. He hadn't asked her about her paintings in a long time.

"Of course," she answered. Her voice was quieter, milder. She brought the painting to the table and uncovered it. He put down his coffee mug, as he was nursing a hangover, and took the painting gingerly in his hands. He looked at it for a long time as she stood next to him feeling naked.

"I'm sorry, Ellie," he said. She thought he was going to say next that he was sorry because he didn't understand it, or her, or anything she thought about or tried to do. "I'm sorry your paintings are so dark. I hope the light in the middle finds a way to grow." He handed the painting back to her, and she took it with a small tremor in her hand. Then her whole body began to shake. Willis stood up and brought her into him, holding her firmly in his arms.

"I'm sorry too, Willis." Her words were barely audible, but he heard her. It was a beginning; reconciliation, a white flag. She didn't care about anything else except being in his arms: this moment, a communication between hearts. Then he unexpectedly pulled his face away to look into her eyes, and leaned in to kiss her with a forgotten softness, which turned into a tremendous mounting force. They stood in the kitchen and devoured each other, filling in months of confusion, silence, and disdain; they clawed their way back to each other. He lifted her swiftly and carried her up the stairs to their room, which had only known short periods of sleep and longer suffering. This time, they took each other mutually, rhythmically; they flowed together beautifully, like the inner workings of a musical instrument that hadn't been touched for a long time—longing to sing again. Her dress seemed to melt away under the warmth of his expert hands. She had been afraid of him for so long—who he had become, how deep his soul and sorrow was buried—she had denied how much she needed him. She freed him of his garments with a clumsy urgency, and they laughed together as he helped her unfasten his belt buckle. Finally, they fell together, baring more than their bodies. This was the first time they had honestly made love to each other. It seemed they had found each other, after all the hiding.

A few weeks later, Ellie made another discovery. She was like clockwork. She waited another day or two and the expectation of spotted blood never came. By the end of the week, she was feeling ill at breakfast and in the afternoon. On the following Saturday, she went to the art gallery and waited for Peter. When he arrived, he held her arm out to her but she didn't take it.

"What's wrong?" he asked.

"I'm not sure I can do this," she said. "Carry on like this, I mean. I think you are hoping that it will become something more and it can't. It just can't."

"I'm not anticipating anything more from you," he said. Although, deep down, he felt wounded; a small pang of embarrassment and disappointment cut him. "Ellie, the art exhibit is next month. You can't back out now. Think of the opportunity—you have a great talent. I don't want you to miss out on this chance to share your work."

"I see the way you look at me, Peter," she said. "I've been flattered by your attention. I've been lonely and foolish." He took her gently, yet firmly by the arm—in earnest—and led her into a corner away from the crowd.

"Don't say that," he insisted. "For the record, you've looked at me the same way—you still do, even now. I know you're lying. There's something more you're not telling me. I know you're married, but I also know that I understand you better than the man you are with. We can make our stamp on the art world together, Ellie—think of it."

"I do, but it's not enough, and it's not right."

"So giving up your passions is the right thing to do?" He wasn't sure if he wanted to kiss her or slap her; something in him wanted to do both.

"I love my husband," Ellie said with conviction. There were tears in her eyes now, which she didn't bother to conceal. In that moment, knowing there was no longer the risk of losing anything, he took her by the shoulders and kissed her long and hard. The breath was drained from her lungs, and for a moment, she was almost convinced she didn't need air to breathe anymore. He slowly pulled away from her and searched her eyes for some spark of hope. Ellie struggled to make her gaze opaque, so that he couldn't see into her soul, although her mouth twitched with emotion. His life seemed focused and uncomplicated, and she had so many variables to reconcile; she would become his only complication if she stayed—if she threw away everything in her life except him and her art. She was now finding a way back to Willis, and there was another piece of the puzzle to work out between them: a baby. Her life would never be her own again. Peter gave her a pained, defeated smile; without uttering a useless goodbye, he fixed his hat and walked away from her. She watched him—the straight line of his back—as he walked rapidly down the stairs and pushed his way out the door, carrying all of that heavy, battered pride to safety.

Chapter 12

That evening, Willis was home and Ellie was grateful. She made dinner and they enjoyed small talk between bites. After the dishes were washed and cleared away, she found him in the living room. She had a drink in her hand and handed it to him.

"I don't need that," he said. She smiled.

"You might," she said, and he raised an eyebrow.

"What would you think of bringing someone else in here to live with us?" she started.

"Hmmm," he said, "it could help with our mortgage."

"Oh no," she laughed. "This person wouldn't be able to pay." Willis looked at his drink and then looked at her and the expression on his face changed rapidly.

"Do you mean?"

"Yes," she said. She wasn't sure yet of what was going through his mind. "Is it good news?"

He put down his drink, leaned over, and held her. He wasn't sure if the timing was right for him, but he knew it was time. He would shape up. He had to—and there couldn't be a better motivation for him.

The next day, the couple went to Ellie's parents' house. They hadn't visited them in a while, mainly because the situation was too tense. Her parents were disappointed that Willis had left Sunny Acres before his treatment was finished, and they were quietly concerned about their daughter's emotional and financial welfare. They couldn't support the newly married couple forever. The welcome wasn't as warm as in days gone by, but Mr. and Mrs. Birch were pleased to see them. Willis and Ellie were ushered into the sitting room by the older couple, and they all sat down.

"How are you both?" Mrs. Birch asked.

"Better, Mother," Ellie replied. Willis gave a smile of confirmation.

"Good," Mr. Birch said. "We have been a little worried about how the two of you have been getting on."

"Thank you for helping us out," Ellie said. Willis nodded. He was trying to swallow his pride, but he also knew things had to change.

"We're just glad to know you are doing alright," Mrs. Birch answered. Her husband looked a little disgruntled, but held his tongue.

"We have some good news," Ellie said. She wanted to move the conversation in a more positive direction.

"Oh?" said Mrs. Birch.

"Well, you two will soon have to get used to being grandparents." Ellie broke the news as quickly and bluntly as possible. She waited for their reaction. The moment lasted for an eternity before Mrs. Birch let her breath go and leaped out of her seat to embrace her daughter.

"Oh, Ellie! How wonderful!" she blurted out and hugged Ellie, who began crying and laughing. Mr. Birch pulled himself out of his armchair slowly and traversed the room to shake Willis' hand. He was not less enthused; he was simply processing it all more slowly and pragmatically. Willis took his hand with appreciation. The circle between them all was being reinforced.

Once the excitement simmered down, Mr. Birch said, "Well, now is the time to start thinking about the future. Willis, do you think you're ready to consider law school now?"

"Yes, of course," Willis answered.

"When is the baby due?" Mrs. Birch asked.

"In the winter," Ellie answered. The two women smiled at each other, while the men gravely absorbed the work that needed to be done.

Chapter 13

One evening, as Ellie was coming to grips with the notion of a person growing inside her body, she was strolling aimlessly up and down the London streets. She thought of how she was in the middle of the world, and the world existed in the middle of her. The sky was losing its sun like a dying peacock, and the shadows seemed to stretch and rubber band away from her, attracted to the darkening horizon. The rain clouds were staying at bay over the sea. She became aware of the heaviness in her shoes, nearly tripping over the cracks in the centuries-old pavement. Her head was floating, somehow detached from her body and the fingertip-sized creature in her belly.

 She turned down a familiar road, either on purpose or by design; she wasn't sure. Ellie drew closer to a large, bright window that emitted happy chatter and light, airy classical music lifting into the grey night. She stopped in her shoes, looking in. She watched the elegant people in their black evening attire sip their flutes of sparkling champagne and mingle in small groups. She was visible in the large window, casting light onto the dim sidewalk where she stood, but they didn't see her. They were in a different world and she couldn't cross over to join them. Her eyes left the elegant people and drifted, falling on the art that adorned the walls—canvases that had become portals of the world. Some were bursting with colour, and others drew darker tones; living snapshots of memory, places, perceptions, emotions that couldn't be expressed in any other medium. The paintings were music for the eye. She was watching the opening night of the art show unfold—Peter's art exhibit.

Then she saw him, shifting in his shoes in the far corner, briefly holding hands with one elegant woman and then another. She watched him anxiously switch his wine glass between his hands, back and forth to create an opening for any patron who approached him—any prospective buyer, admirer, art lover, romantic partner. He looked like a boy trying to find the right person to engage in a slow dance. She watched him as he watched everyone else take in his heart's work. He was about to turn his head to peer out into the evening—the other world that didn't revolve around him yet. Ellie instinctively moved back, away from the window, acutely aware that she could be inside with him, basking in that moment of sunshine. She pulled herself away and walked briskly down the street towards the train station, towards home, back into the monotony of the world she knew. She could feel a silver cord deep down into her body pulling her back, to an insistent unborn cry; the creature she could not ignore, dwelling inside as she fought to stifle her own desperate cry deep in her throat. She had to contain the universe existing under her skin.

Chapter 14

As the months went by, Willis organized his submission papers for the law program at Cambridge with the help of his father-in-law, and Ellie focused on her painting and taking it easy. She had found a weekly art class, which she reveled in and where she met other like-minded people. She was happy. Willis had also curbed his drinking and was able to cut down on his sleep and anxiety medication. He committed to regular doctor checkups to stay on track with his well-being, and their family doctor gave him a commendation for his improved efforts.

He maintained his friendship with Sam, which became a healthy connection. Sam was motivated and he encouraged Willis to keep moving forward; he had found work at a textiles mill and was able to land Willis a position there as well. This new opportunity allowed Willis to begin saving for the future and cover their immediate needs. He was eager to move his in-laws slowly out of the picture. He was the head of his own family and tired of feeling patronized. He would listen to the conversations between his coworkers; they had their own gripes and bumps in the road, but all in all, their lives seemed to run relatively smoothly. They talked about normal family stuff—how their kids were doing or that their wives spent too much on new dresses. He felt these men were a healthy model for him.

For a while, he had felt like he was on the outside. A few of the men were older, although some of them had fought in the war. The subject seldom came up. It was a question, or a given, and then left alone. The younger men were straight out of high school and full of piss and vinegar, but they were honest workers and liked to keep things light. They all worked well together, with only a few minor incidents where they butted heads, grinding their horns. Willis observed that the men with families and who had come back from the war seemed to be balancing their work and personal lives well, and quietly reconciling whatever lurked in their pasts and haunted them now; they had found some secret, a purpose. They had also readily welcomed Willis, and Sam was there to help show him the ropes and bring him into the fold. Willis felt an affinity with his coworkers and place of work. He even got along well with the female employees, although they mostly kept to their own groups, sharing gossip and tittering about things that were in female code and, therefore, impenetrable to men. Once in a while, the younger men would whistle at the ladies on the worksite and were greeted with eyes that cast daggers or, in rare cases, looks of open appreciation. There was an unsaid harmony and understanding between the sexes at the workplace, but clear lines that were not to be crossed.

One day Willis overheard one of the men saying, under his breath, how the women should be back in their kitchens and not taking the jobs of the men returning from the battlefield. Willis immediately took the man forcibly aside and pointedly told him that the women had every right to earn a pay cheque to help support themselves and their families and weren't meant to be kitchen slaves, and if he had a problem with that, maybe they could figure it out after work. The other man muttered something unintelligible and scuttled off, after giving him a dirty look, and then Willis caught the eye of a young woman who had overheard them. She gave him a small smile and quickly moved on, back to her station.

The textiles mill was an anchor for him; there was a sense of steadiness, meaning, regulation, and retribution. He believed he was making a contribution in the world, helping people, and making a positive difference after being a part of so much destruction. Willis began taking control of the present and shedding the burdens of his mental barriers: his guilt, inferiority complex, vices, and procrastination. He was relieved to see Ellie happy, pursuing her passions, glowing, and nesting.

In late autumn, Ellie was growing rounder. She was in her sixth month and every person who passed her on the street felt compelled to place their hands on her growing belly. She welcomed them, although it still felt strange, as though her own identity was already vanishing and she was merely seen as a vessel for this new life: a mother-to-be. One morning after Willis had already left for work, Ellie struggled to get out of bed—then a sharp pain sliced through her abdomen. She noticed blood on her nightgown and jumped up to find blood on the bed sheets as well. In a panic and doubled over, she slowly made her way to the phone and dialed the operator for her doctor. An ambulance came quickly to the house and her parents and Willis were contacted soon after to let them know she was in the hospital. When Willis got the news at work, he rushed to the hospital and found out her room number; unfortunately, he was a few steps behind her parents, who were already at her bedside. Her mother was holding her hand, and her father hovered a small distance from the bed, looking forlorn and helpless. He acknowledged Willis with an accusing glance that said, *What kept you? You should have been here first*, as he rocketed into the room. Maybe Willis was being paranoid, riddled by his own guilt, for not getting to the hospital sooner. He had the car that day, but traffic was thick. He was sure he saw something in his father-in-law's glance, though, something that said, *How could you let this happen?* Ellie's doctor came into the room and breezed past Willis before he could even get to his wife. Ellie focused on what the doctor was telling her, while the rest of them focused on Ellie. Willis subconsciously felt the cigarette pack in his jacket pocket and desperately wanted to escape the room to have a puff, make it all vanish away with the smoke. Hospitals made him twitchy now.

"Mrs. Hancocks, I'm so sorry to tell you that you've had a miscarriage. We are still going to have to deliver your baby—you will be brought to the delivery room shortly." The doctor was a young man. He was stoic, but not entirely unsympathetic. He then nodded respectfully to the other people in the room and left them all to grieve. Ellie burst into tears. She was secretly grateful to have her parents closer to the bed; she wasn't ready to look Willis in the eyes. She didn't want to face any of them, but her parents were acting as a buffer to the growing fear of sharing this loss with the person who had invested just as much. She felt like a failure, and she didn't believe in misery loving company. Her thoughts were also going inwards, into protective mode, as she prepared herself for the delivery, separation, and loss.

Willis didn't understand why her parents wouldn't leave the room, even for a short reprieve, to allow them to talk, cry, and absorb this tragedy together. This was their loss—yes, it extended to her parents, but he needed to be with his wife. Didn't she need *him*? Ellie wasn't giving her parents any cue to give her space or time to think, or just be. Soon, the attendants came to wheel her into the emergency room—Willis and her parents were firmly told to remain in the waiting area.

For Ellie, the delivery room was filled with people dressed in blue gowns and wearing surgical masks and shower caps.

"Everything will be fine, Mrs. Hancocks," she was told. Then a plastic mask was placed over her mouth and nose as she was told to breathe normally and count to ten. When she woke up, she felt a great emptiness. She had to say goodbye to someone she had never met. A nurse asked her if she would like to hold her baby, and her first thought was *why?* She thought it was a strange cruelty, but the nurse insisted it may help her to heal in the long run. She was told to sleep first, and then the baby could be brought in. When she woke up again, Willis was at her side, watching her with a strange look in his eyes. He looked torn: happy to be near her, but terrified to be alone with her; happy she was okay, yet knowing she may not be okay ever again. Both of them were trying to make sense of something that had no answers. He didn't say anything; instead, he just sat beside her, laid his hand her arm, and let his eyes shimmer with tears. He was still there when the nurse brought in their baby: a boy. He was completely swaddled, save for a small opening that framed his eyes, cheeks, and mouth—a pale shade of blue. He was almost too tiny to hold, but otherwise, he looked perfect. He was the one intact, while Ellie and Willis were looking upon him, tentatively touching his soft blanket and cool skin, were the ones who broke apart.

Chapter 15

Willis turned back to the bottle; he couldn't breach the gap that had ripped through his marriage. The alcohol, the addiction in him, was like a beacon on the shore; whenever the waves were turbulent, it brought him to some place calm and familiar, even though he knew it was distorting his world and slowly killing him. The sleeping pills followed, and he grooved out his old impression in the couch. Ellie had grown thorns all over her body overnight; she was silent and distant, untouchable. The plans for starting his law program in the coming fall were put on hold, once again, as he struggled to pull himself back out of the hole. He managed to hold on to his job at the textiles mill, and he and Ellie existed like two ghosts in the house. Eventually, he began sleeping in the same bed with her—it was an unsaid truce where he made the initiation and she didn't kick him out—but was careful not to so much as touch her feet under the sheets.

For the next five years, Willis continued to work at the textiles mill at minimum wage. He made a habit of carousing at the tavern with Sam after work, drinking away his pay cheques, flirting with the waitresses, and dancing with random women. There were a few loose girls he took out behind the building, and Sam turned a blind eye. On occasion, Sam would also bring Willis home to Ellie in the wee hours of the morning, stinking drunk. She would quietly let him in with a tired, pained look on her face, shaking her head and casting a disapproving eye on Sam. In her mind, he was the bad influence, the instigator. She didn't want to acknowledge the pain she and her husband shared—it was a poor excuse to justify Willis' behavior; he was only making things worse.

Ellie retreated back to her art. She had maintained her friendships with the ladies she met at the art classes she took years before. She taught a few classes at the community art center, which gave her some purpose and lifted her spirits. Many of her girlfriends had children now and continued to grow their families, and her heart broke to see each child come into the world and grow into a bright, spirited, intelligent little being. She was also painfully aware that her clock was ticking. She was in her late twenties now. If she wasn't married, she might have been considered an old maid; and now she was beginning to feel herself drying up. Eventually, she mustered the courage to bring up the subject of trying to conceive again. At first Willis was reluctant, but he realized how much it meant to her and also thought of how it might mend their marriage. He thought a baby might also help mend him: he had sunk to a dark dungeon, another world he kept secret from Ellie. Their relationship was holding on by a stretched thread. He had turned back to the drink to drown the demons and to prostitutes to assuage the primal need in him.

"Alright," Willis said to Ellie as she spoke to him with tears in her eyes about wanting to try for a baby again. She didn't wrap her arms around him. She simply nodded, as though they had just made a business agreement. How would they ever be able to spark a new life when they couldn't make a spark between them? Over the next two years, they tried until they were tired of trying; then it happened. Only, the spark didn't last. Early on in the pregnancy, Ellie suffered another miscarriage. Now the hole was so dark they couldn't see each other anymore, and they were trapped down there together. She threw all of her tears into a bottomless well, and her anger was thrown at her canvas. She gave birth to a myriad of paintings of babies, dark, bleeding, dangling from ropes, blue, crying, floating up to heaven, and buried deep in the ground. Once the paintings were dry, she covered them with sheets. They were for her to invest in, love, hate, and endure alone. Ellie and Willis continued to dig at the walls, trying to tunnel their way out, or up, and always in different directions.

In 1956 Ellie's father approached Willis at his work one day, while he was on lunch break. Mr. Birch had strolled into the mill and called Willis out like he was his boss.

"Willis, son, let's go for a walk. I need to have a word with you." Right in front of his mates, who looked at Willis with a question in their eyes asking, *Do you need back up?* Willis waved them away with a cocky smile and followed his father-in-law outside.

"What do you mean coming in here … ?" he started.

"What do you mean being such a jackass? I won't stand for it, Willis."

"Pardon, sir?"

He told Willis that he had seen him escort a young, trampy looking girl into a hotel downtown. Willis visibly stiffened, wondering if he knew how many trampy girls there had been in recent years. He also knew about Willis' alcoholism; he could see the slight tremor in his hand and the paradox of nervousness and over confidence in him. Willis had an answer for everything, a way of deflecting the reality of his life situation.

"Don't play dumb with me, son. I know you've been through a rough time, but there is no excuse for your behavior. I also know you and Ellie have had your problems, but she deserves better." Mr. Birch pushed out his chest, looking down at him. He wasn't a big man, but he was a force to be reckoned with. "I saw you in downtown London going into a cheap hotel with some poor floosy. Listen, your ... marital life ... is none of my business, but the welfare of my daughter is my business."

"Well, you've been taking care of our welfare for some time now, so I suppose you should be an expert." Willis shot back. He was painted into a corner, and his only defense was to come out swinging.

"I wanted to talk to you about that, too. I don't want to support the two of you—I never have wanted to, to be honest. You might feel like a failure, but I feel like a schmuck. Especially when I can't see things getting any better and my son-in-law won't man up and take care of his wife and responsibilities."

"I'm working, aren't I?"

"Cut the shit. This is a job, but it's not getting you any further ahead."

"A job is still a job, and this is noble work," Willis protested. He could feel his face getting hot.

"What you don't know is this *job* is a dead end, not to mention a health hazard, and it only pays you enough to support your drinking—yeah, I figured that out too. Working? You're escaping in this place—running from everything else and telling yourself you're doing something worthwhile. Right now I pay for your house and groceries; Ellie may as well be living at home with us. That can change, you know? You have a choice here."

"What choice is that?" Willis sounded sullen.

"You can enroll in the law program like we discussed before. If you do, I'll pay your tuition. If you don't, I'll tell Ellie about your infidelities and advise her to divorce you. I won't have her married to a philandering bum. If you make a change and decide to shape up and find some direction in your life, I'll help you do that. If not,

I beg you—don't pull Ellie down with you." Mr. Birch was stern and his proposition was cold cut, but his intentions were sincere. Willis glared at him, feeling trapped and invaded; he didn't want his life to be in a fishbowl. However, he did care for Ellie and he knew that his father-in-law's brutal words were spoken with truth, and a good heart: a father's love. Yes, he was blackmailing him, but he was also protecting his sole treasure—his daughter.

"Alright," Willis said. His shoulders sagged slightly as Mr. Birch extended his hands to pat them.

Chapter 16

In September 1958 Willis boarded the train to Cambridge. It took him a while to wean himself off the crutch of alcohol and prepare his submissions for entry into the law program. His coworkers at the mill ribbed him a little about trying to rise above the crowd, saying he would come out of his fancy school thinking he was better than everybody else, but they gave him a warm, memorable farewell lunch, secretly envious of the road he was embarking on.

Ellie had come out of her own darkness to help support him, as she wanted him to succeed and for them to build a new life. She had resigned herself to the notion that they may never know the joy of having children, but she didn't want to lose him altogether. Willis felt empowered, having his wife beside him in his hour of need. There was the possibility of a way out, and they didn't want to lose sight of it. They knew that they could never return to the place of intimacy or trust they had known before, but they were supportive of each other and committed to their bondage as husband and wife, no matter how twisted or battered.

"I'll be home every weekend," he assured his wife, who stood on the platform she'd stood on years before, trying to smile through her brimming tears.

"I know," she said. "Study hard, darling! I'm proud of you!" He kissed her goodbye on the cheek and then disappeared behind the door, appearing again a moment later to wave at her from the window seat. The train heaved a heavy sigh and began to slowly chug away down the track. He had mixed feelings about leaving her and reminded himself that he was doing this for both of them. He was also looking forward to spending time with Sam. His friend had enrolled at Cambridge a year earlier on the GI bill and was taking general courses. He had asked Willis to go with him but was met with hostility. Willis was stunted and angry. The suggestion of Sam receiving help from Mr. Birch to pave his way had faded away long ago. Willis quietly admired Sam's determination to put his nose to the grindstone and get to Cambridge on his own steam. The mill was a tad lonelier without him; however, Willis had dug in his heels and carried on. At the time, he was too far down in the hole to care about much. Sam's absence was one more knot in the rope.

Although many years had marched by, the transition from military to civilian life was not an easy one, and they both still understood the agonies of waking up in the middle of the night with memories of the war playing in their heads like a movie reel. Ellie had tried to assuage him with glasses of water and motherly kisses, which were comforting but had brief effects. There was no remedy, not even time, Willis feared. Willis switched his focus again, like a train switching tracks, as he laid his head back against the passenger seat. He was getting better at pushing down distressing thoughts.

Willis arrived at Cambridge dragging his luggage behind him. Sam, who had caught the train from his parents' home in York, met him at the campus. Sam had decided to stay at his parents' house over the summer to save his pennies for the next semester's tuition. In the end, in light of Willis' agreement to embark on his academic journey, Mr. Birch relented to helping Sam enroll in the law program as well. Part of his decision was based on Sam's excellent grade point average during his first year, so he pulled a few strings. He didn't know much about Sam, but the young man had made a good impression on him years before at the wedding. Mr. Birch also knew it would be good for Willis to have a close companion with him, someone to help keep him on track. There was no animosity from Sam about having to make his own way in the first year without Willis; he enjoyed the first year on his own, dipping his toes in the academic waters and adjusting to campus life. However, he was anxious to share the experience with his friend. There were young students and older professors everywhere, eager to store up books in their minds and exchange ideas. This was a foreign, protective world, a nest or safety zone from the harsher realities where they could each learn to fly.

Sam spotted Willis entering the front lawn that was lined with an army of trees, and he bounded toward him. The day was overcast, which made the historical buildings seem more severe.

"We're here!" Sam exclaimed. His own luggage was slung over one shoulder like an army bundle. Willis grinned. He was grateful to have a friend with him.

The two men tried to sign up as roommates, but were sent to different dorms, due to the lack of available lodgings. So they met each morning in the cafeteria for coffee before a long day of lectures. Upon Mr. Birch's generous offer to help him enroll in the law program, Sam had decided to enroll in the introductory law courses and follow suit with his friend. Willis wondered if his friend was nervous about what discipline to major in and the thought of continuing to roam through the university classes alone or if he did hold a genuine interest in the law profession. It was clear that Sam did not have the best aptitude for law, and Willis tried to push him and spent evenings in the library drilling him on the material. For Willis, law was a natural calling, and he took well to his classes and professors. Sam teased him that he hoisted his arm in the air so often he might get a cramp. He wasn't afraid to make mistakes either. Usually, he was correct, but he thrived on the class debate when he was off target too. Sam quietly made notes, his hand always moving, and seldom raised in class participation. He was the observer, the recorder, and the silent sponge. He would often expose his thoughts about theory and practice to Willis in the evening hours, and Willis urged him to bring forth his points in class. Slowly, Sam began to test his voice in the arena, posing questions about the stark differences and grey areas in the practice of law between countries and governments, and the professor welcomed his exploration of ideas. He began to gain confidence and become an equal study partner for Willis. He also managed to keep up in his English literature classes, where he had a found a rare passion.

As promised, Willis returned home to Ellie every weekend. Her father paid for his travel expenses. She had downsized from their rented house and found a spacious two-bedroom, street level flat, which she decorated with her own paintings and simple pieces of furniture. It was a place they could afford to own and call home: a new home to begin a new life. Two pieces of her art had a significant effect on him—one hung in the hallway: an impressionist painting of a battle scene where a small crowd of young men in civilian clothes and red army helmets stood with rifles in an urban street setting. This was the painting that had been her last project at Cambridge. She titled the painting *Revolt*. The other painting hung in their bedroom: a woman in a white wedding dress and veil holding a magical wand in one hand and a bouquet of red roses in the other. She reminded him of Glinda the Good Witch from *The Wizard of Oz*. She was alone at the altar, placed on a single cloud with a faint rainbow in the background. She looked determined and hopeful, not sad. The colour red disturbed Willis now, but he tried to praise her work and not ask too many questions. He didn't want to upset her during their visits. It was easier to keep everything on the surface.

The couple was in want of nothing, it seemed, and life moved along at a happy pace. He studied hard throughout the week so that he wouldn't have to compromise their time together. She also prepared meals in advance, so they would dine on leftovers for those two days and spend more time in the bedroom or taking long walks through the neighbourhood and nearby parks. They didn't venture into the hustle and bustle of downtown London. They were focused on reconnecting and piecing their marriage back together. They discussed their future plans, such as Willis' ambitions to start a law practice, but Willis didn't want to bring up the prospect of children again until his studies were complete. He had three years left before graduation. If possible, this time, he wanted to make sure they were financially established before starting a family. Ellie had managed to sell a few of her paintings, which contributed to their income and made her happy. They were both pursuing their dreams. He thought, *Why spoil things?*

In December 1961, the second-to-last year of his studies, Willis came home before the Christmas break, after taking his exams, to collapse in the arms of his wife from mental exhaustion, empty his mind, and enjoy the holiday. Ellie met him at the station as usual, but said little on the drive home in their secondhand car. He was too tired to notice or ask if anything was amiss, although he sensed that she was tense. When they parked the car and got inside the door, she took his coat and hat and hung them up gingerly on the coat rack, transforming it into a thin man. She clasped her hands in resignation.

"I have some news, Willis," she said. "I'm pregnant." He watched her eyes carefully, hesitant to touch her, as the hardwood floor suddenly shifted under his feet.

Chapter 17

In the new year, since she'd broken the news, Willis dreaded coming home for the weekends. First, she would smother him, then yell at him, break into crying fits, and eventually throw up or become too exhausted to do anything. She was near the end of her first trimester. It wasn't something he kept track of, but she was adamant in reminding him. She was no longer the sweet and demure young lady he had once imagined during his time away at war. He realized that he wasn't ready for these changes and future responsibilities, and maybe she wasn't ready either, no matter how much she thought she wanted a baby. Willis had begun to think the miscarriages were a blessing in disguise. He wasn't convinced anymore that they were meant to be parents. He needed the space and concentration necessary to complete his studies and would often retreat to the small den in their flat, closing the door, only to be interrupted regularly by his wife's mood swings. One minute she was offering to bring him a cup of tea, the next minute she was complaining that he was neglecting her. He was thankful that his weekend stays were short, and he was always eager to get back to his classes. He also dreaded the last day he spent with his wife ... not because he would miss her, but because she would become incredibly attentive, bordering on clingy, and apologetic for her eruptions during his visit. She blamed everything on the pregnancy. Her roller-coaster of emotions drained him of all compassion and inspiration. He felt suffocated around her, and he could only imagine what his life would be like once the baby arrived. At the end of the long trip back to school, Sam was a breath of fresh air.

On one particular trip when Sam met him at the train station, ready to drive him back to the campus, Willis answered his unsaid question by simply rolling his eyes.

"It's that bad?" Sam asked with a raised eyebrow.

"She's a mess," Willis replied. "This wasn't supposed to happen now. Not yet." Sam would pat his friend on the shoulder, and no more was mentioned about her. Secretly, although Sam was concerned for his friend, he also felt a pang of sympathy for Ellie. She was alone in every sense.

Willis worried about being able to support his wife and new baby. He knew that her parents would be able to help them, but he felt uneasy about leaning on them again. He felt weak. He was supposed to be the man of the house and take care of everything. He was also disappointed that Ellie would not be able to continue working on her paintings. She was so ambitious about her art, and now she could barely raise her paintbrush. He hated seeing her helplessly abandon her dreams. She had a gift. The baby would change everything in their life and everything between them. He didn't even know his wife anymore—perhaps he never had in the first place. He was afraid of a lifetime of being cooped up in their flat with his wife and baby, and then more babies. He thought he might go mad. Since the beginning, as a newly married couple and near strangers, they hadn't had a chance to properly connect and adjust to the challenges of married life; there were too many obstacles to overcome.

He wasn't sure if he had found his partner in life or if he had simply been hormonal, hasty, and not willing to look beyond what was offered to him.

A telegram arrived from Willis' father that read:

MOM DIED. COME HOME.

His father didn't have a lot of money to throw around, and telegrams were costly, especially when sent overseas. Although he was completing his second-to-last year of law school, he was allowed a couple months' hiatus. He knew that he could afford to take some time for a family emergency; he was a serious student and his grades would hold. However, Ellie wasn't as forgiving. Willis had been hiding from his parents all of these years, as much as from anyone else. He hadn't kept his promise of bringing his wife to Canada, and she was in no condition to make the trip this time. Besides, it was too late for his mother. He had not been close to his parents, but it was never their fault. He wasn't running from them—he was running from himself, whoever he was in that present moment, always, believing there was a better existence behind the next corner and chasing the phantom dream ahead of him. He could never see that the place he was in was the better place. He understood that now, and the least he could do was to be there for his father in this lonely time. Ellie didn't understand—she felt that he was abandoning her and choosing a lost parent over the chance to share the beginning of a new life's journey. He wanted to remind her that the new life was not safe in their arms yet, but he didn't have the heart; it would be salt in a wound that would always be fresh.

He bought his passage ticket, and on the day of his departure, he told Ellie that she had her parents nearby, that this was something he needed to do for his father and the memory of his mother;

he couldn't venture into fatherhood without mending his relationship with his own father. Willis told her he had broken things to mend and something to learn.

He didn't tell his father when he would be arriving, and when he reached the St. Lawrence, he then hopped on a train and made his way across the prairies and through the Rockies to his small, rural hometown in British Columbia, just outside Vancouver. When his father opened the door to his farm house, his body became rigid in shock. He looked haggard and was wearing a lumberjack shirt and slacks with suspenders. Then he reached out his arm and pulled Willis into his chest with force.

"Son," he said simply. There was a faint light in his eyes; he seemed transformed and was no longer the grim, stern man Willis remembered, the man who grumbled, hidden behind his newspaper as though it were a shield of truth, spouting his unfounded beliefs about the state of the world. Willis felt his arms move around his father, a natural reflex or an act inspired by something else.

"Hello, Father."

"Come in, by God. Do you want some coffee?"

"Sure, Father. I'll make some," Willis offered.

"No, come in and sit down. I'll make it." Willis' sister Ivy breezed into the room and grabbed the coffee pot, already holding it under the running cold water tap.

"Ivy," Willis started.

"Hello, little brother. How was your trip?" Ivy said. There was an icy tone in her voice that didn't go unnoticed.

"Fine, I guess." Willis said. "Are you here alone?"

"No, my husband came with me. Where is your wife? We are all so anxious to meet her."

"Pregnant. She couldn't make the trip," Willis answered. Ivy turned off the tap and kept her hand from shaking. A jolt had shot through her body as she stood at the sink, trying to stay composed. She kept her secret—her own dream of bearing children—locked in her heart. The dream still eluded her. Ivy also watched from the corner of her eye how her father greeted Willis, his hand still on his son's arm as though touching him kept Willis in the room and made him real. She and her husband had been greeted warmly enough, but it was as though they had returned from a holiday; their arrival was welcomed and appreciated, but somehow, she also felt it was expected. It was true that she had stayed at home longer and come back more often, but it was a daughter's duty to come in the wake of her mother's death. Willis' arrival was a gift. The thought made her flinty and jagged.

"Milk?" she interrupted their chatter. It was mainly her father who was babbling exuberantly; Willis was a happy distraction for him; that she was pleased to see. She had not been able to bring him the same light, the same comfort, even though she had been the dutiful daughter who wrote home and kept her parents informed. Ivy felt torn; the kitchen counter was a barrier between her and the men in her family.

"Uh, yes, thank you," Willis answered, trying to simultaneously follow the news of the town that his father was rambling about: the young boys who had returned and started families, the start up at the old lumber mill, the booming industry, one young girl in the neighbourhood his mother had tried to set him up with and how she had married and now had three kids and one on the way. The words were becoming nervous filler and avoidance from talking about why they were all there—brought back from great distances—in the familiar kitchen that would have been silent otherwise.

"Sugar?" Ivy asked.

"Yes."

"How many cubes?" She could hear the abruptness in her voice. She wanted the focus to be on her, and she couldn't explain the reason for it. She wanted to interject, be involved and appreciated for more than just being the daughter and sister in the room, the lamp, the coat hanger, the one making the coffee. Before Willis could answer more than an incoherent "uh," it was her father who turned to her.

"For God's sake, Ivy, who cares about how much sugar? One sugar, two sugars, no sugar—just make the coffee. Your dear brother is home! You're both home!" Then he stopped, as though he had lost his place. "Your poor mother would have given anything to see you together." He wept silently while Ivy and Willis looked on, stunned and helpless and mildly ashamed. Willis laid a hand on his shoulder, and his father grabbed it and wiped his eyes with his free arm. Ivy didn't know what to do—she was too far away. She quietly placed a cube of sugar in the coffee cup, stirred it, and placed it on the table beside Willis. Then she poured a small glass of port for her father. When death came, one always drank port to help drown the bitterness. He took the glass gently in his palm, wrapping his thin fingers around it, and brought it up to his lips, sipping the alcohol with a long-cast meditation in his eyes. He was seeing her, drinking to her, remembering her. When the last drop was gone, he placed the glass back on the table. The three empty people sat adjacent to each other, strangers searching for a common ground: there was only one person who linked them together, and she was gone.

"Thank you, both, for coming home. I think I'm going to lie down for a while." His children respectfully moved out of the way, with their hands turned out, ready to catch him if needed. He took on his frail self again—the brief spurt of energy gone, sucked out of him. The reality was sinking into his bones: his children were home, but only for a short time. His love, his constant, was gone. Every room felt cold now. Willis and Ivy watched their father leave and strangely felt him take the room's warmth with him—he embodied the spirit of the old house.

"How is your coffee?" she asked. They sat down at the table again. Willis took a sip.

"It's coffee," he answered. "It's fine."

"I feel Mother is here," she said suddenly. "She'll take care of him." He wasn't sure how to respond or what his thoughts were on that subject.

"When was the last time you were here?" he asked. He didn't want to speculate on spirits taking care of the living; he wanted to talk about things that were concrete: people, skin and bone and pumping blood, time and numbers, things he could call tangible and was able to measure.

"Two Christmases ago—didn't you get our letter? Did they not mention it in their card as well?"

"Maybe," Willis shrugged. "Probably—I don't remember." For a second he wanted to confide in his estranged sister about the rough waters he had been through and the rapids ahead. How everything had become a blur, but she seemed to guess already.

"You've kept yourself away for a long time—none of us could reach you, could we?" she said sadly. "We've just missed you, Willis—to the point of not knowing you. I'm sorry it took mother's passing for you to come." There was sharpness in her voice, and a hint of pity, which stung him. He was going to say something in protest, but Ivy's husband strode into the room. Willis was partly relieved to be kept from saying what wasn't yet formed on the tip of his tongue.

"Ah, the prodigal son returns!" Ivy's husband stretched out his arm to greet Willis and added, "so to speak." Ivy shot him an annoyed look and he instinctively tried to retract his flippant comment and cleared his throat. Willis took the other man's hand with a squint in his eye. "Sorry mate," he yammered. "John Sourdough. Good to finally meet you—shame it's under these circumstances."

John looked at his wife sheepishly. It was a genuine icebreaker, and after all, his father-in-law had talked only of Willis since they arrived. Funny, the boy he had nearly turned his back on because he had decided to join the forces was now the hero son who had survived it all. The fact that he was also the son who had become an emotional recluse and never bothered to write home was irrelevant. Honestly, John was sick of hearing his father-in-law praise him to the heavens and his wife complain about his first place status in the family. They nearly threw her a party when she got married and announced that she was moving overseas. It didn't matter who she married or where she was or what she did with her life; it only mattered that she was finally out of their house and doing something somewhere else with somebody. The double-edged sword cut through her and then wrenched its way out again, ready for another stabbing, tearing both ways.

"Oh, that's alright, and you must be the unfortunate man Ivy finally persuaded to marry her," Willis shot back without missing a beat. He was about to add "poor sod," but thought better of it. He had already fired a shot at both of them, and he felt instant regret as well. What were they doing? "Now that all that's out of the way, how about you sit down. Let's talk." Willis pushed out the seat opposite him with his foot. Ivy's husband took the back of the chair and angled it before sitting down. Ivy rolled her eyes and left the room, saying something about finishing a chapter in her book.

"Listen," Willis began, "I know I've been a jackass."

"Are we in a confessional box?" John smirked. "You don't have to explain yourself to me. I don't know what there is or isn't between you and Ivy or the rest of your family, but I think there's a lot that they don't understand."

"Did you enlist?"

"I saw everything from a distance," John admitted. "I was an ambulance driver. So I saw my share, but I was really just there to help clean up the mess and get the boys out of harm's way and to higher ground."

"Right."

"I hear you were in the front lines—lucky to make it out."

"Did I make it out?" Willis asked. "Some days I'm not so sure." John stood up and went to the icebox. He pulled out a beer.

"You want one?" He asked Willis, but before he could answer, a bottle was passed into his hand.

"How long are you two staying?"

"Well, we've been here for a couple of months already. The funeral is in two days. I think we'll be leaving the day after it's all done." He took a swig. "Damn shame. She wasn't very old. In her sixties, was she?"

"Turning sixty next month," Willis said. His brother-in-law shook his head.

"Damn shame."

Willis was anxious to turn the conversation again. "So, you're an entrepreneur—a tycoon-type, eh? What are you interested in?"

"Anything that has the possibility of turning a buck." John sat up straight and puffed out his chest slightly. "You know, since the war, there is a lot of opportunity to start from scratch, a chance to build up again and rekindle new ideas, like the phoenix rising out of the ashes. It's a great time for idea men like me to start up new businesses. There's stuff you might not even think about too, like plastics and automation, making parts to build bigger parts. Everyone wants something that will make their lives easier; it's just a matter of finding out what it is, building it, and then convincing people that it is something they do need." Willis thought he was talking about building air out of air, but he bit his tongue and nodded. He must have been on to something, because he and his sister seemed to be doing alright.

That evening, as Willis passed their bedroom, the door was ajar and he overheard them talking.

"Are you sure you're feeling alright?" John asked.

"You mean besides how I should be feeling about my mother's funeral?"

"You know what I mean. Do you need anything?"

"I just need to stop talking about it. I'll be—fine." Ivy grunted. "Where are those damn pills?" She was rustling through her bag with one arm, the other one wrapped around her abdomen.

"Hang on, I'll get them." Her husband sounded agitated. Willis could hear her sister muffle a cry, but it didn't sound like a cry from pain, at least not from physical pain.

"Why does this keep happening to me? What's wrong with me?"

"Try not to do that," her husband said. "There's nothing wrong." Willis quietly kept moving past the door. His heart felt heavy; he had never heard his sister in distress, never seen her in an intimate light. He was acutely aware that he would probably never know what their conversation was about, what pain they bore between them.

On the morning of his mother's funeral, the sky was grey with threatening rain clouds. The service was held in the small church down the road, which his parents had dutifully attended. Willis felt hesitant to be there. He had fallen out with God, or whatever he thought he used to believe. The minister prattled on about the impermanence of life and the eternity of heaven, describing his mother as being free and at peace with everyone she had ever loved and lost. He said that she was waiting for all of them to join her. Willis watched all the sad, solemn people around him, nodding, dabbing their eyes. How could the minister tell them about what happened after? How could he know? Willis shifted uncomfortably in the pew. His mother lay at the front of the room, open casket. Was that her wish or something his father had requested because he wasn't ready to shut the lid on her quite yet? What would she have thought? What did she want? Did anyone care to ask?

In all fairness, there hadn't been much time when she was diagnosed with cancer, and she had fought her battle until the end. He knew his mother, even if he hadn't been around to see her for years—she wouldn't want to dwell on it. Whenever there was bad news or some trauma to face, she would close the door on it, turn the topic. Life was too short for tears, she would say. She probably didn't let his father prepare for the end either. Maybe she thought she was doing him a favour. Why cry over something that couldn't be stopped? *Just live, be here with me, trust in God and know I'm going somewhere and you'll follow soon.* He could hear her words as though she were sitting beside him trying to bring some hard love comfort, even now, after everything, words that never fell on his ears when she was living; he heard these words nonetheless. He somehow knew that she must have told his father something similar—to prepare him and comfort herself about the end, not knowing if it would be a dark, black curtain or some strange transformation. Would she become the butterfly after the long cocoon?

Hymns filled the small church, but his lips didn't move. He couldn't participate in words that he didn't believe entirely; he had his own quiet goodbye for her, something not shared. When the service was over, the mourners were invited, if they wished, to pay their last respects. Those who had endured enough went into a separate room to drink tea, eat baked goods, and talk about things that concerned the living, still tethered to this world. Some just went home or perhaps elsewhere. Willis felt obliged to look into the coffin, and as the line got closer and he could see her small, prone body more clearly, he felt his throat tighten; his heart felt as though a human hand were squeezing it as he moved closer to death. He had seen enough of death, but somehow his mother's death seemed more cruel and senseless than what he had witnessed on the battlefield. They had signed up for death; they knew it was a possibility. His mother had been backstabbed by death, sideswiped out of the corner of her peripheral vision; death found her in her quiet house while she continued to care for her husband's needs after she had raised her children and watched them leave her. She didn't smoke and barely drank, as far as he knew, but death still found her before she expected and then it made her wait. He felt his fist clench.

When he finally had his turn to look down into her resting place, he noticed that her face was smooth. He wasn't sure if it was the touch of makeup, to make her more presentable for the mourners, to remind people of how they knew her in life, and for the pending afterlife, but every worry line was gone. He wondered if her soul was also rid of all worry. Then he felt a strong hand on his right shoulder and turned to see his father pulling him back into the land of the living. He looked relieved, at peace. Now they had to give her back to the earth. Not everything had been said yet, but they had sent her on her journey.

"Do you want to go back to the house now?" his father asked.

"What about everyone here?"

"I've already spoken to most people—some here, some who have come by—I gave my thanks to the minister. I don't want to stay. I told him I don't want to watch her go into the ground. He seemed to understand. I'm tired. I've been saying goodbye to her for months. I want to go back to the house now, spend time with you and your sister. Let's go," he said. His eyes were dry. The burden of death seemed to lift at the end, as though a gift from those departed. The mounting sadness replaced by sheer exhaustion, and then the eventual and sudden remembrance to live on, to not waste the purpose of self, a gift for the departed, an understanding. If people are fortunate, the living usually helps them get there. It is a circle. Willis nodded at his father and quietly left his mother's side, but not before reaching in to touch her cold hand.

Ivy caught his eye across the room. She looked distracted, as an older friend of her mother's chatted senselessly, attempting to console her with words or anecdotes that meant nothing. She looked over and could see they were leaving the church and a relieved expression washed over her face, a means of rescue. Willis watched her hastily pat the woman's hand, and then she grabbed her husband's hand. John looked like an awkward wallflower, despite Ivy's attentiveness to introduce him to the people she knew. The tired couple made strides to meet Willis and his father before they reached the door.

"How are you doing, Dad?" she asked.

"I'm alright. Just ready to go," he said.

"Let's get back to the house and make some tea," she offered.

"Sounds good," Willis said. They were leaving as a family, in the protective shadow of their mother and wife. In the house, they mainly stayed in the kitchen area, staying close and saying little. They engaged in small talk and listened to their father's stories and ramblings, careful to not make the air too heavy, but also not filling it with idle words that didn't match the weight of the day. Ivy made a simple dinner and they sat around the table, chewing thoughtfully and drinking beer. The port was put away; it had served its use. After dinner was finished and the dishes were done, Ivy announced that she was going to turn in, as they were catching the train the next morning. She gave her father a quick kiss on the temple. Her husband stood up, shook hands with the men, who he felt were closer to being called family than before the trip, and left the room to retire to the upstairs quarters. He squeezed Ivy's hand quickly as he brushed by her, and Willis saw her give him a look of thanks and a quiet promise that she would join him in a minute. Then she turned her eyes on Willis and motioned to him with a swift, small jerk of her head. He obliged and met her just outside the kitchen threshold.

"You'll take care of him, won't you?" she asked. It was a strong request, a concern. "How long will you stay then?"

"He'll be alright. I will help make sure he's coping with it all and that he's settled before I leave," he assured her. "I'll stay for a month or so. It will take that long to get the bills settled and line up some long-term help."

"They've got good neighbours," she said. "He won't be alone." Then she caught herself and rubbed her forehead—*they* no longer existed. "He has good friends."

"Try not to worry," he said.

"Willis, what I said before about you not being here ..."

"Forget that; you were right. I wasn't. I haven't been—I can't change it."

"You did what you thought was right," she said. He knew she meant enlisting in the army. He wanted to argue that it *was* right, but now wasn't the time to go down that road again—not in the same kitchen where it had all exploded in the first place, the room where his mother tried to not worry about her son and instead focused on the constancy of meals and dishes.

"The past few years have been … complicated," he said. It was feeble.

"It always is," she dismissed. He wasn't sure if she meant life in general or that something complicated always prevented him from being where he should be. He chose not to read too deeply into her comment, as much as it niggled at him. He had enough to think about.

"I suppose so," he said, not sure of what he was agreeing with.

"We don't have to be friends, Willis. We're grownups now," she carried on. "We didn't have to be friends when we were both living under this roof, for that matter. That isn't what this is about. You have your own matters to tend to."

"I didn't always see the bigger picture, Ivy."

"No, you just saw the pieces where you thought you fit. It doesn't matter now."

"It doesn't have to be that way."

"What does matter is that you're here now, for Dad. I don't expect any more than that. Whatever peace you need to make, you can do that now." Suddenly, Ivy was a woman in front of him—a hard-shelled woman who wasn't afraid to speak and who could see more of what was going on inside him than anyone else. He felt a sibling bond that he hadn't acknowledged before, a likeness of minds and vulnerability to pain. She was carrying something deep in her, and somehow, she could see the same in him. Still, they didn't know each other's secrets—only that they were there. "If Mother is watching, then you've made your peace with her too. You came. That really is all that matters. I had no right to get on you about the rest—anything you did or didn't do before. That's your business. I was glad to see you, Willis. Give Ellie our best." She somehow knew that would be complicated too. They both knew that they wouldn't be ringing each other for friendly visits when they returned home to England. A white flag was raised, but they were still awkward strangers, being civil for the sake of their parents. There was too much water under the bridge, too many regrets, distances, and quiet grudges to bridge the gap.

"Thank you, Ivy. Safe trip tomorrow then," he said. "John is a good man. I'm happy for you." She nodded and headed upstairs to turn in and be with her husband. Willis stepped back into the kitchen to see his father staring at the drop of beer left in his glass. He raised the glass to an invisible person sitting in the opposite chair and quietly swallowed the rest of it down.

Chapter 18

Ellie lived with her thoughts and the quiet, imaginary conversations with her unborn child. She was still processing Willis' absence—whether it was a genuine need of his to connect with his blood family or another reason to flee. She assured the small human inside her, as much as she did the insecure woman in herself, that he was only gone for a short time; he would be back to make everything right. She had to remind herself daily, hourly, that she was telling their child the truth. He loved them, he wanted them—he had to put something in his heart to rest, and then he would come home and make them whole again. Her thoughts were weapons against the drowning doubt, which was only exacerbated by the influence of her parents. He had left her to defend both of them, thrown her into the lion's den. As soon as he left, he had forgotten to close the back door—to sear the hole in her heart—and her parents had swooped down into that place of uncertainty like vultures. Within a day of his departure, she found them in her kitchen, helping themselves to cups of tea and burrowing into her head.

"Really, darling, I can't believe he would go and leave you in this fragile time after all those years when he barely even spoke of his parents," her mother sneered. She shook her head disapprovingly as she lifted the thin-lipped cup to her red mouth.

"His mother died. It was right for him to go and pay his respects and to make sure his father was managing alright," Ellie replied. She allowed a bite to her tone of voice, but just on the edge of coy. As much as she despised being trapped between her husband and her parents, she held tightly to the spark of defense for her husband; still, she was painfully aware that she needed her parents' support in her maternal state. She didn't want to skin noses, but she also wanted to let them know that she had a firm footing and there were certain lines drawn in the dirt.

"Imagine not coming to your own son's wedding—there must have been more going on," her father chimed in.

"Don't you remember how rushed we were? We felt we had waited long enough; we couldn't wait for an overseas ship to arrive," Ellie laughed incredulously. "He wrote to them and told them we would visit—then it all went awry. It wasn't his fault."

"It wasn't your fault either," her mother said.

"I know." Ellie gave her mother a hard look. Her mother sighed as though she was the one exhausted from fighting.

"He's a nice boy, Ellie. We've always thought he was a nice boy," she started. "We're just not sure he was ready to be a husband. You must feel it."

"You don't know what I feel—or what he feels," Ellie said. She could feel a quiet rage building inside.

"Do you know what he feels?" her mother shot back. Her father lingered uncomfortably in the background, leaning his back against the counter with a cup of tea in his hand that she hadn't offered him. They were in her space, in her kitchen, and in her head; they had not yet penetrated her heart, and instinctively, she placed a protective, possessive hand on her belly. This child, this home, belonged to her and Willis, not to them.

"I know he's coming back to us," she hissed. Her mother looked at her as though she was ten years old and stupid. Then she shifted her gaze to her husband, knowingly, as they shared an unspoken communication; they were saying to each other, *We tried—she won't listen; she'll learn the hard way.* For a moment, all at once, she envied and resented the bond between her parents, the secret wavelength they shared. It seemed they were showing her what a solid couple looked like—they were a force not to be trifled with: *see dear, this is what you don't have right now—your partner with you, supporting you, making life plans, sharing your unsaid thoughts.* There was a tether, a meeting of minds; she wondered if it had been learned or if there was a cosmic design in the merging of their paths. Perhaps Ellie and Willis' paths had been off their course just enough to intersect, but only by accident; perhaps they were forging a road that was never meant to be. She had to struggle to keep those thoughts out of her heart; she worried such thinking would penetrate to their baby.

"I'm sorry, but I think that you both need to leave now."

"You should find a way to be happy, Ellie. That is all we want for you," her father said weakly. She knew he was only trying to calm the tension. Her mother was already halfway out the door. She had to go out into the fresh air, cool her heels.

Unfortunately, her parents didn't let it lie. Their visits didn't cease—and neither did their persistence. Her mother even went so far as to mention past flames from her university days and to suggest that she should look those men up to find out if they were available. Her father visibly rolled his eyes behind his wife's back. There was a distinct line between giving advice and inflicting malice, and her mother was boldly crossing that line. Ellie had to keep her rage in check, and the bile from coming up in her throat. She wanted to claw her mother to shreds. For her own sanity, and to make a passive-aggressive statement, Ellie began finding ways to make their visits shorter: she had a friend to meet, she needed to do her grocery shopping, or she simply felt tired. Her parents were acutely aware of her condition and seemed to back off more readily if she made any complaint about fatigue or illness. They didn't want to risk subjecting any undue stress on their grandchild. Ellie felt a bit sheepish at times, using her unborn child as a tactic or weapon against the arrows of questions or nagging her parents unloaded on her. Still, there were many times when her fatigue and headaches did get the better of her, and she was all too happy to have the quiet reprieve of an empty house. Other times, she would slip out after her parents were gone and spend her day roaming around the city. The exercise was good for her, and she needed to get out of the confining walls of her living space.

Oftentimes, she would find herself heading toward the National Art Gallery, like it was a homing beacon; she wasn't sure if it was a direction she had consciously chosen or if it was the tiny human in the driving seat who decided which direction she should be going. The sidewalk fell away under her flat-soled feet, leading her back to a place of familiarity, comfort, and possibility. She went there to delve back into the paintings—her passion and past life; she didn't expect to see him, although she couldn't stop her memory from wandering down that path, reverting back to him. Then, one day, he was there. He spotted her first, and some sensation on her neck, some tingling that she couldn't explain, made her turn her head in his direction. She was standing by a pillar, far back from the crowd of patrons trudging slowly through the gallery. As he came over to her, she could already see the world was different. He had a small child, a girl, propped high up on his shoulders. Ellie smiled at him, and to herself—the workings of fate and circumstance. He held the young girl's legs firmly, but with a gentle grasp as she bounced above his head like an angel over him.

"Ellie!" he shouted. He seemed new, transformed, and bright; the toddler, his small daughter, giggled and pointed at the works of art all around her. She knew it was his daughter. The bond between them was too great; they were fused together in trust and love. They were both beaming, and Ellie felt her own smile widen at the sight of them.

"Peter, how wonderful to see you!" she exclaimed and took his free hand, giving it a quick, friendly squeeze. Then his hand retreated to the small leg, keeping the little girl's light balance. She was all that mattered in this moment, but some strange energy seemed to pass between him and Ellie, as though time had suddenly folded in on itself. This spot, near the entrance of the art gallery, all too tender, but time heals all wounds, and this too had passed. There was no animosity, no strangeness—just a realization of time and fate, an alignment in the stars.

"You're in for an incredible ride!" Peter smiled and Ellie felt herself blush. "This little monkey is Madelaine. We call her Maddy."

"Hello, Maddy!" Ellie said warmly. "You must have the best view from up there!" The little girl's eyes dazzled; they were ocean blue like her father's. There was an entire universe forming in those eyes.

"Hello," the little girl said shyly. She was tenderly fidgeting with her father's hair.

"She's just turned three and thinks she knows everything." Peter grinned.

Maddy smiled distractedly then turned her head and shouted, "Mommy!"

"I'm so happy for you, Ellie," Peter said hastily. There was earnestness in his eyes, trying to make her understand a certain forgiveness, gratefulness. She was meant to let him go so that he could have the life he found. There was no time for anything else, and Ellie was partly relieved to not feel obliged to tell him about her twisting roads: her attempt to keep art in her life and to pull together the threads of her marriage and stitch them into place. This chance meeting wasn't about her; it was about seeing him and a lesson for her to realize that she had let something go for a good cause. Then she noticed a petite, brunette woman come into her peripheral and sidle up beside Peter. There were no guarantees she might have been this woman on his arm—she might have only prevented the true happiness from coming into his life.

"Hello there." the other woman smiled brightly. They were all bright little stars, shining in front of her. Ellie marveled at how this woman didn't even know who she was—how she factored into their lives or not—and still she came into her space with such warmth and welcoming. There was solidness in their circle of three, soon to be four, as she noticed the other woman's round belly protruding from her thin frame.

"Ellie, this is my amazing wife, Beverly." Peter announced, gazing proudly at the petite woman. Beverly smiled sheepishly with one supportive hand on her belly. Peter reached over and rubbed her baby bump, gently and protectively.

"It is so nice to meet you, Beverly," Ellie said. "Congratulations!"

"Same to you, on both counts," Beverly replied. "When are you due?"

"I'm four months in," Ellie said. "And you?"

"Sooner than you, I'm afraid," Beverly laughed nervously. "Our next little bundle should arrive in two months' time, if he or she decides to stay put for that long."

"You have a beautiful little girl," Ellie offered.

"Thank you. She's a handful," Beverly said. "I'm hoping this one will be easy; I'm a bit nervous about chasing after two little hellions."

"You'll be fine." Ellie smiled at the picture Beverly painted; at the same time, she was calming her own fears of caring for her firstborn.

"Thank you. I'm sure you will be, too. You'll find out what I mean soon enough—it is a learning curve bringing these humans into the world. You think you can place all of your influences on them, but they have their own little minds and personalities from day one, and it doesn't take them long to figure out that they are their own little people. It's a journey about guiding them to be good people; don't think for one second you can control everything they do or how they think!" Peter placed a hand on his wife's shoulder, and Beverly stopped herself. "Oh, don't take advice from another pregnant lady—it's the hormones and lack of sleep talking. Every mother is different and so is every baby; the two of you will figure it out together."

However, Beverly's description of motherhood rocked Ellie; she hadn't thought about the creature aspect of raising a baby; she couldn't get past the idea of delivering the baby, never mind being responsible for shaping the kind of person her baby would become or possibly was already. She smiled at the other woman weakly.

"It was wonderful to see you again, Peter. I really do need to run off and finish my errands. Lovely to meet you, Beverly—I hope everything goes well," Ellie stammered. She felt like a strange, misplaced piece in a puzzle box, and the cover on the front of the box depicted a perfect family—the family in front of her.

"Take care, Ellie. Best of luck to you," Peter replied, and they began to drift away from her with their arms around each other. Madelaine had grown bored with the adult conversation and was humming a sweet little tune to herself; Ellie wasn't sure if it was a tune she faintly recognized or something this airy little girl had conjured. The sound drifted away from her as they moved farther into the art gallery, and Ellie watched with her heart half-buoyant, half-breaking in her chest.

Chapter 19

The house felt strange the next morning when Willis descended the stairs to the kitchen, although there had hardly been any hustle and bustle with Ivy and her husband there. He was concerned that his father would wake up to the emptiness, knowing that his wife wasn't coming back. Willis wondered if he would feel the same way, in the end, if Ellie went first. They already lived like ghosts and had become accustomed to their hidden thoughts and heartaches. He wondered again if a baby might change them, force them back into the light somehow. Willis clung to the railing on the stairs as he made his way down to the kitchen. He was surprised to find that his father was already up, sipping delicately from a strong cup of coffee. Willis looked at the small, blue, budding flowers on the walls.

"Good morning, Father," Willis said groggily.

"I just made a pot. Help yourself," his father answered. Willis poured himself a cup and joined him at the table. They drank their strong coffee in silence until his father felt the need to speak again. "Crisp, bright day out there," he said. "I think I'll plough the field."

"Why don't you take a day?" Willis asked. "I'll take care of that for you."

"You?" his father chuckled hoarsely. "You haven't been on that tractor since you were a teenager ... and only then you did it to keep us off your back, or impress the girls, I'm sure." He winked at him knowingly.

"I never tried to impress any of the girls around here," Willis scoffed. "No matter how much mom wanted me to set my eyes on somebody in town."

"Yes, your mother." He looked pensive. "She did worry about you." His brow looked heavy, and Willis wanted desperately to change the subject, but then his father raised his eyebrows just as quickly and set onto something else. "You turned out alright in the end!" he exclaimed with a half-hearted smile, slapping Willis lightly on the back. His father left the room to get dressed and took his coffee cup with him. Willis could hear him singing an old familiar tune as he washed his face in the small bathroom. He didn't know if he should be more concerned that his father seemed to be carrying on alright. Was he still wearing his thick, protective armour and trudging through the day to just get through another day? Perhaps, but Willis also had the queer sense that his mother was still lingering and giving him words of comfort, just as Ivy had speculated. He looked around at the neatly organized cabinets, the special plates propped up on the high shelves, and the chinaware on display in the small, glass cabinet. The colours she must have picked out with excitement in her nesting flurry.

He drained his coffee cup, put on his jacket and cap, and headed out to plough the small field for planting the spring vegetables. As he drove the tractor up and down the field, he watched the soil turn under the wheels and began to think about his own seed growing inside Ellie, and the others that never made it, like a bad crop. He wondered about his inability to father those stunted babies and how, perhaps, it was for the best. Then he turned to dark thoughts about the possibility of this seed surviving—was it something that wasn't really meant to be? He tried to turn his mind back to the present—the field ploughed, ready for planting, and the high sun beating down on him. When he was finished, he went back in the house and peeked into his father's bedroom. The old man was snoring in his bed. One day away from everything would be good for him.

Willis closed the door gently and left the house. He walked until he came across the old town sawmill and stood watching the young men from a distance. Their burnished muscles heaved the lumber planks to the shed, while far in the back the heavier work was happening—bringing the logs out from the water, then swinging and towing the massive fallen trunks onto the mill for straightening and sawing. They were well-paid for their blue-collar efforts, and the community thrived from the lumber industry; new houses and businesses meant more families and a better economy. Willis wondered at what he had walked away from—he knew his ambitions had driven him away from the small town and its people; front porch philosophers. However, he suddenly felt, again, as though he had sold his soul for something of a lesser value. What was the path he had been meant to take, and what path was he now obliged to trudge down? He turned away from the work site and wandered the town a while longer. Then he made his way back to his family home. When he climbed the porch steps, he noticed the sun was behind him, leaving long shadows. His father was standing at the stove throwing together bangers and mash. Willis reached into the fridge and grabbed a beer for him, placing it next to the stove, marveling at this man who seemed to be completely self-sufficient, even in his loss—perhaps more so. He had never seen his father cook dinner when he was growing up, as though it was a poor example to allow a man to do the "women's work." His father seemed to read his mind.

"She felt diminished somehow if I even suggested she sit down and have a beer while I make dinner. She would scoff at me and say, 'What would the neighbours think?'" he laughed. "I always thought,

'What neighbours?' She was so worried about what everyone else thought all the time. If you ask me, how you live in your house is nobody's business but your own! Screw the conventions!'

"The world isn't changing very quickly, is it?" Willis said.

"Well, it's changed quickly enough. Perhaps that's why so many cling to the old-fashioned ideas, but that's just what they are. Old-fashioned. What happens to the poor sods that lose their wives and then can't even boil an egg for themselves? It's ridiculous. You meet in the middle, you share the work, that's how you survive; it's all about respect, self-preservation, and learning how to live together."

"I don't think I've learned that one yet," Willis said out loud. His father turned away from the stove and frowned slightly at his son.

"How are things with that wife of yours?" he asked. He sounded vague, but there was something tense in his voice, something close to the surface. "You said she was pregnant?"

Willis didn't want to admit too much. He grabbed a beer for himself and cracked it open as his father dished up their supper and carried the plates over with cutlery in hand. They sat down to eat.

"I'm sorry we never made it out here. We've had a rough time of it the past few years."

"I understand," his father said. "Your mother didn't, but I did. It's a great distance and it's hard. It takes time to settle the dust when you first get married. It's like learning a dance, isn't it? For the first while, all you do is step on each other's toes, and then you find your rhythm."

"We're still learning where our feet go." Willis smiled. Then he decided to change the subject. "When did Ivy and her husband arrive?" he asked. John had told him, but he wanted to hear more of the story from his father.

"They were here for a couple of months. Your sister handled the last stage of your mother's illness the best—she and your mother seemed to share a secret understanding; they grew closer than they ever had before. I was no help. All I could do was hold her hand, bring her tea, and look at her with troubled eyes. She told me to the leave the room most of the time, told me to go and rest. I didn't want to rest. I didn't want to leave her for a second. She passed away while I was out of the room—I think she planned it that way," his father rambled. "She wouldn't let me say goodbye to her—never the actual word *goodbye*. She didn't want to hear it."

"So Ivy knew she was sick?"

"Yes, your mother wrote to her close to the end and she came right away."

"Why didn't anyone write me then?" Willis asked. His father gave him a surprised look and even seemed a bit staunch suddenly.

"Ivy kept us in the fold and abreast of what was going on in her life. She wrote frequently and came over the pond to visit when she could. You didn't exactly contact us for anything, did you? You were gone, doing your own thing. We understood, as much as we were forced to understand. Your mother missed you terribly, you were here son after all, but if she felt pushed out, she was the last woman who would ever try to push herself back in," he replied. "She didn't want to make you worry either. Not that far away, not if you didn't even bother to write or come home or think about us at all. She loved you enough to simply let you go, knowing you had been returned safe from the war—that was enough to keep her going, to know that you were in the world, even if you weren't in her world anymore."

Willis felt a strong wave of guilt wash over him. His father was right—he had been so busy chasing shadows, forging paths, and killing his demons that he hadn't bothered to reach back to the place and people he had come from. He watched as his father solemnly rinsed his plate and left it in the sink.

WILLIS' MOTHER

The day we drove to see the doctor, I seemed to be holding my breath all the way there while sitting in the passenger seat of our old car. I was watching the fields and thinking about how everything would be coming up new in a few months. I already felt in my body that I might not be here to see the new crop, but instead, I would help to push up the next one. It was a dark, cynical thought, but oddly enough, it secretly made me laugh. Actually, I must have laughed out loud because my husband looked at me funny. I'm sure he thinks I'm going mad. To be honest, I'm sure he's always thought I was going mad, but was too polite to say so. Bless him. I knew what the doctor would say, or at least I was preparing for the worst; the body tends to do that—to protect itself from some inevitable thing. Like a baby crying in the night, it lets you know something is wrong. There is a strange vibration that occurs before disaster strikes. My husband didn't want to accept it. When the doctor said the words "cancer" and "terminal" in the same sentence, my head was reeling and my heart seemed to stop then, but I also had this strange thought that said very clearly "you already knew this." In fact, I felt the tension go out of my shoulders, as though I was being validated for the first time—the truth spoken out loud meant I wasn't going mad from guessing. On the drive back home, I put my hand over his on the steering wheel. We were going down the road together. "You're going there, too." I said. "I'm just going to win the race, that's all." To my surprise, he gave me a funny smile. Then he started to cry—a quiet kind of crying. I kept my hand on his to help steer us home.

The first thing I did was crack open a beer. Not very ladylike, but I didn't care anymore. The world didn't have to know—it was something for me. Then I sat down at my little roll-top desk and began writing a letter to Ivy. I knew the tone of my letter was straightforward, the way I would talk if she were sitting across from me. I told her I had terminal cancer and was only given a few months. I asked her to come and visit us and to bring her husband if it was possible. I knew I needed family around me. I wanted to write to Willis as well, but I found it difficult to bring pen to paper in the same way. The door to his world, his life, seemed to be closed to the size of a pinhole; I missed him terribly, but I didn't know him anymore. I didn't know the man who had come back from that terrible war. I didn't know anything about his life. It was selfish, but I had enough to deal with coming to terms with my own end; I wasn't sure I could bear taking on whatever dwelt in the dark well of him. I know that I would want to absorb his darkness too, but it might prove to be too much for me. So, in all those years, I mailed only one letter to congratulate him on his marriage and let him know how glad I was that he had come back in one piece. Then I kept silent. If Ivy decided to share the news of my illness, then fate would bring him to me. If not, I didn't want to burden either of us unnecessarily; perhaps neither one of us can be saved. She didn't tell him, in the end, and perhaps it was just as well. I will take him with me, locked in my cold, full, tired heart, to the other side.

When Ivy and her husband came, my heart felt lighter and heavier at the same time. I didn't want my child to watch me die, but I needed the flesh of my flesh with me to be reminded of what I accomplished in my life and that I would not truly be gone. There were two people I brought into this world, and at least one of them would help see me out. It was an inexplicable comfort to me. Also, I wanted to tether myself to her for the short time we had together. My husband didn't know what to do, except shuffle around me morosely—and drink. I remember hiding all the alcohol in our house when he returned from the Great War, so that the monster in him wouldn't surface, then for a short time after Willis left us. Now, all these decades later, I had to do the same thing again. I wanted him to be with me—sober and present with me. Once again, I was being selfish, not letting him grieve while I was still alive. Ivy confided in me about her heartbreaks, the unborn children she mourned. I told her a child would come to her one day, perhaps in an unexpected way, but that she would come to know the responsibility and sacrifice of being a mother.

I also confided in her my fears, as well as my curiosity, about death. When would it come? How? What would death look like? Would I be aware of anything that was happening? Would it be a dark veil or like slipping into a dream or warm water? Would death be kind? I wanted to share these fears and notions of death with my husband, but I didn't want him to dwell on death before it was time. I would be able to talk with him openly if he was more accepting of it and able to look at this figure of death coming for me in a philosophical way, not like an intruder in the night or a physical assault on both of us. I can't stand him looking at me like I am already gone from him: he looks at me with the same face I'm sure he will have when he watches my casket lowered into the ground. I can't look into that face; I can't spend my last days that way. I told him I needed him to see me now and feel me now. I needed him to live with me in my last days as though we would be alive forever. He couldn't do it.

    Soon, I was confined to my bed, the one I knew I would be in when I slipped into my last dream. Ivy and I would talk for hours about the past, present, her future, my next journey, and even Willis from what we could speculate. Often, I would catch my husband hovering just outside the door—I would see him through the crack in the doorway, left ajar. He looked like a lost child. He couldn't cross over to my side, whatever side I was on; I had one foot in, but I was still here. I am speaking of myself in the past tense now, as I feel this passing in me. My daughter is at my bedside—her poor husband feeling out of place in a house with death in its walls. I had the gift, the opportunity to bond with her as a woman; my children have been gone from me for so long.

    She came back to me and sacrificed herself to take me into my final stages; she made sure I was clean, fed, and comfortable—spoon-feeding me soup and changing my soiled pants—everything I once did for her and her brother. She gave me the ultimate gift of reciprocation, of gratitude. She gave me the secrets of her heart and brought our lives full circle: mother to child to mother, and I am the child again. I tried to not feel humiliation or regret while she did these things. Sometimes that was when we would have our most intimate conversations, to shift the attention away from the greater act of love happening, the messiness and magnitude of fully taking care of another human being. How do nurses do this? How do they shift their brain to take care of someone else's mother in that extent? Ivy was my nurse, my heart, the witness to my demise. My husband couldn't bear it. He couldn't handle much beyond changing a child's diaper and holding my hair out of my face if I was sick from drinking too much. I don't blame *him. He wouldn't be horrible at getting down to the primal nuts and bolts of caring for a spouse—the grittiness of it—I just wouldn't be able to bear him either, and I don't know why. We've bared everything we are to each other, but this is new territory. He is in this house with me, and that is enough. He is downstairs grappling with a loss that will come soon, his and mine. I understand, I pity, I forgive, and I love. Until this time, as I can feel the darkness creeping slowly toward my heart, I hold on to one truth—I was still here.*

Chapter 20

The next morning, Willis woke with a heavy heart. The past was coming back to greet him, and what he once thought was true in his mind was shifting rapidly. He thought he had escaped from a small town populated with small-minded people, including his own family. The truth was, he did need to spread his wings and see more of the world and what was really happening beyond his hometown, but he didn't need to burn his bridges. He had won a war, but he had lost the one that mattered most; worst of all, he was the only one fighting. He couldn't reach into the earth or the clouds to hold his mother again, tell her he was sorry and that he loved her. However, he did have an opportunity to make everything right with his father and face what he couldn't face before.

He rose out of bed and got ready for the day, which was brisk and bright. His father slept through breakfast, so he made scrambled eggs and drank his coffee and then headed back out to the field to sow the seeds. In the afternoon, he went into town to stock up on the week's groceries, as he noticed supplies were dwindling in the cupboard and ice box. In the grocery store, he spotted one of the women his mother had once tried to set him up with—she caught his eye and immediately came over to him. As she approached him, he noticed she had three children in tow. She was also pregnant. He could feel his innards tighten, and he wasn't sure why. They weren't his kids, but the thought of anyone having more than one child made him dizzy and ill.

"Willis! You're home!" she exclaimed. He was almost sure the entire store heard her, and he was ready to bolt for the door. She looked primped and fresh, save the discernible greyish sags under her eyes. Then her tone changed in a heartbeat, "I am so sorry about your mother."

"Oh, thank you. It's alright. Yes, I am helping out my father. It's so nice to see you again," he stammered.

"You don't remember my name, do you?" she raised an eyebrow and gave him a flirty smile.

"I'm sorry, you're right. I don't." He wanted the earth to swallow him or a giant wave to carry him out of the door. He felt abashed, and again, he wasn't sure why. A short while ago, he wouldn't have cared that he couldn't remember one of the girls that his mother had paraded into their house and who he had considered as "small-minded" all those years before.

"It's alright." She shrugged. "It was a silly schoolgirl crush on the boy next door. You're mother meant well. It was uncomfortable, I know."

"So, I see you've moved on and gotten over that crush," he said, switching gears, referring to the three clean, bright-eyed little beasts hanging off of her.

"Well, yes," she started. "The father of my oldest child thought he needed to save the world too. He marched off to stop the wave of Communism. Only, he didn't come back." She forced back a tear and stroked the heads of her children. "I remarried, though. Now I have these angels as well."

"I'm so sorry," he said again. He felt foolish and, for a strange moment, wished he could change places with her deceased husband.

"Thank you," she said. "I'm so glad you're home, Willis. Take care of yourself." She turned and ushered her children out the door, with a grocery bag tucked under one arm. He wanted to swoop in and help her with her grocery bag, but he didn't want to interfere.

Over the next week, he helped his father sort out his financial affairs. There wasn't much to go through—his mother had a small clause in her will leaving all of her worldly goods to him, which didn't mean much. She didn't truly own anything; everything was in both of their names: the house and farm. It was more a sense of going through the motions, the formalities of death and letting go. When they left the small law office, his father turned to him and said, "She left me her heart." Then he scooped his frail, old body into the driver's seat of the old car and opened the passenger door for him, and they drove down the dusty road toward home.

Later, after they looked over his father's bills and bank statements and squared everything away, the two men sat at the kitchen table and quietly ate dinner together. Then his father stood up with a sudden determination and announced, "We need something." Willis was startled, not sure what his father was on about, and watched him go to a cupboard under the sink and dig around in the back—his arm reappeared with a large bottle of whisky attached to it. "She didn't think I knew about this," he chuckled, almost malevolently. There was a guttural happiness or satisfaction in his throat. His father stroked the bottle with a strange grimace on his face then brought it over and set it on the table with a victorious thud.

"Dad," Willis protested.

"After you went away, I got a bit carried away," he said. "She hid this from me, trying to save me from my own sorrow. No, it's different now. I need this. I need to have a proper drink with my son." He brought two glasses to the table, unscrewed the bottle, and poured them each two fingers. His father took a healthy swig and then asked him pointedly, "So, tell me about this little wife of yours. How did you two meet?"

"I met her while I was on leave in London in the fall of '44," Willis said. He sounded matter-of-fact and there was no wistfulness in his voice. His father frowned at him.

"You love her, don't you?" The older man raised an eyebrow, studying his son. Willis bristled at the blatant implication that he didn't.

"Sure," he said. "Of course I do. She's my wife." He squirmed.

"That doesn't mean a hill of beans—whether or not you're married has nothing to do with it. Love doesn't just stick around because you live under the same roof and have a piece of paper with both of your names on it," his father sniffed.

"We've had our problems," Willis replied. He was starting to relent; at first his defense had fired him up, but then he saw it was useless. This was the time to be transparent: his chance to be with his own flesh and blood and be honest.

"What kind of problems? Nothing too serious, I hope."

"Serious enough for me to stay away all of this time—to not want to burden you and Mom with everything I was trying to sort out." Willis took a sip of whisky and swirled the remainder in his glass, his mind half a world away. "I'm sorry I got married in such a damn hurry and that we didn't make it out this way like I had promised."

"Well, don't get me wrong, I would have loved to see you and meet your new bride, but it was your mother who was more disappointed," his father said. Willis gave him a slightly hurt look, which made his father chuckle a little. "I know how new and difficult marriage can be in the beginning, and you had just come back from the gallows of hell to boot. I understood you needed time to plant your feet again. So, tell me, did you plant them?"

"I'm still working on it," Willis replied. He felt his father's steady gaze on him and then he turned to look him squarely in the eye. "I shouldn't have married her, Dad, and I don't mean *her*. I shouldn't have married anyone."

"Why not, son?"

"You said it yourself—I just returned from the gallows of hell, the belly of the beast. I wanted to move on with something that had meaning and purpose as quickly as possible. I didn't take the time to put things back together, to clear my head. I just wanted something that I thought made sense. I was in a dark place." Willis was near tears and he wasn't sure if it was the effect of the whisky, frustration with himself, the feeling of being interrogated by his father—albeit with gentle and compassionate probing—or all of the above. He hadn't realized it was all so close to the surface.

"Son, listen to me. Listen to your old man. You will always have dark days—it doesn't matter if you've been through a war or not; life can be a battleground. What matters most is that you trust the person who is beside you and let them help you. If you can do that, then you know you are in a true marriage." He pointed his finger at him. "I've been there, you know."

"What are you talking about?"

"I've been there. I never wanted you to know it. I fought in the Great War, the First World War. We thought that would be the end of it, but it was only the first tremor before the earthquake. I marched off proud, too, thinking I was going to save us all." His voice faltered. "You're more like your old man than you think." Willis felt another wave of guilt wash over him.

"You kept that inside you all these years?"

"I only kept it from you and your sister. Your mother was the one who rescued me—told me that I shouldn't try to block it all out, but she reminded me that I was here and we had to move forward and bring you both up to be self-sufficient human beings. We had a job to do—a job we loved. Slowly, over time, that other world and all of its harrowing memories floated into the back scenery. They never disappeared; they never will, but I'm still here and so are you." His father took another swig. "It's time to move forward, Willis." In that moment, Willis believed his father was talking to him as much as talking to himself. A quiet reminder spoken aloud and it was just as true for his father now that his mother was gone. The two men sat together, absorbing and bridging.

"I don't think I am ready to be a father. The thought of being responsible for someone else's life scares the hell out of me," Willis said. "The idea of being a father has never been a priority for me."

"No man is ever prepared to be a father—just like no woman can truly be prepared to be a mother," his father said. "Children are gifts that you never regret, and you can't send them back." Willis smiled grimly at his father's words.

"I don't like the idea of bringing them into this world," he said.

"The world can change. Think about it. What better way to move forward and be thankful for your life than to live forever through the future generations?" his father rebutted. "You have the great opportunity and responsibility to pass a part of yourself on to another bright, hopeful being. Don't waste that opportunity or look at it as a curse." His father stared at him, hard, as Willis gazed into his empty glass, pretending not to feel his father's eyes boring into him.

"How did you do it, Dad?" Willis asked. "How did you bring us into an uncertain world and pretend to forget what you knew—the dangers, the madness of the human race?" His father stiffened slightly, mostly at being called "Dad." His son hadn't been this close, in proximity or endearment, in so many years. He cleared his throat.

"It was my responsibility to be there for you. To protect you, teach you, and show you a better world."

"I understand now why you were so much against the war."

"I was silently proud of you; I was also afraid for you. I was angry that the world had to endure another war—and for a cause so far away. I didn't want you to see what I had to see."

"If the Germans won, we would have all been prisoners," Willis refuted. "Besides, there have always been wars. The human race can't seem to thrive without them, for one reason or another; for territory, for belief, for honour or wealth. It doesn't matter. There will always be wars in this world."

"I know. I know all of that, son. I just didn't want those tragedies to encroach on *our* world, the life I'd built to protect you and steer away from all of those horrible memories. I knew what you would be marching into, and I didn't have the guts to tell you. I didn't want you to be part of it—to have that weight on your shoulders. I was also selfish, we both were. We were scared of losing you for that cause."

"It is okay, Dad." Willis took his father's hand. "I'm here. We won. It's okay. The world is better now." Then his father gave him a strange look.

"I'm okay too. I'll be okay here without your mother," he said. "Now it is time to go home and be with your wife. You've been here for a month, son, and I appreciate it. Now you need to get back to your life. You need to be witness to the beginning of your child and to be there for Ellie. It is an incredible journey that you don't want to miss."

Willis held his father's gaze and an overwhelming emotion overtook him; he did something that surprised them both—he leaned over and kissed his father on the cheek. He felt absolved. He was also deeply envious of the deep, beautiful relationship his mother and father had shared—he wasn't convinced that he and Ellie would reach that place of complete oneness, and now there was a child coming into their frayed existence. Still, he needed to try and to hold his father's words close. Willis nodded.

"Okay, Dad," he said. Two simple words that held a promise he wanted desperately to keep. He held his father, wondering if it could be for the last time; then he climbed the stairs to his childhood bedroom, in this house that used to be his own, packed his belongings, and slept past sunrise. In the morning, he ate breakfast with his father—they were both solemn, but more connected and healed by all that had passed between them. Willis washed the dishes and then put on his jacket and hat, picked up his suitcase, and left the old house with his father standing in the doorway alone, watching him leave again—his frail arm hanging high in the air.

Chapter 21

When Willis returned, he was relieved and terrified to find that Ellie was still round with their unborn child. Her belly was like a beach ball; he felt drawn to her, but also was distinctly aware of the barrier this baby already created between them. He also felt his in-laws had grown seasonably cooler toward him, and he couldn't fathom the reason why.

The months flew by, and the baby was born, a boy, who they decided to name Willis. Willis Sr. found himself studying the baby's face, looking for traces of his own features, and then immediately felt guilty. Ellie was a sweet girl. She wouldn't do that. How could he think that? He felt a strange mix of relief and disappointment. Still, part of him wanted the baby to belong to someone else. He was running from both of them, but he couldn't run far. He couldn't leave. He was too dependent on her father's generous coverage of his tuition. He hated being dependent on anyone for anything.

He also pitied this baby that wasn't supposed to arrive yet. This baby he didn't have time to take care of and for whom he wasn't about to rearrange his life. His home visits stayed the same, except there was even less sex, if that was possible, and more time spent hiding in his small den. Ellie didn't meet him at the train station anymore. He would hail a taxi to the flat, in the sun, rain, wind, or snow, and be greeted at the front door by his unkempt wife bouncing a crying baby on her chest and covered in spit-up. Inwardly, he recoiled. He didn't bother to lean in for a kiss. Surprisingly, she never seemed to notice.

"Hi," she said curtly upon one of his arrivals and stepped away from the door to let him in. He walked in with a grimace on his face and put down his suitcase in the front hall. His son had stopped crying, but examined his father warily from the safety of his mother's shoulder, as though he had to reassess who this strange man was all over again. They were strangers too. Willis Sr. stroked the baby's head briefly and then addressed his wife.

"How about a cup of coffee?" he asked.

"Sounds good," she replied. "I would love a cup." He grimaced again, but her back was turned.

"Fine."

"Problem?" she asked, alarmed by his flat tone. Still, she was distracted.

"No, of course not," he replied. He went to the cupboard, and she retreated to the nursery, cooing to Willis Jr. He rolled up his sleeves with purpose and brewed the coffee, slowly breathing in the dark, rich, sweet aroma. He felt his nerves relax, one by one. The baby whimpers in the other room had subsided, and his wife reappeared trying vainly to fix her hair. She stood close to him and breathed in the coffee as well. He felt a sudden tenderness toward her, not being able to fathom her sacrifices and constant work to take care of their baby. She smiled at him, but it seemed she was smiling more at herself.

"He's asleep," she said simply and victoriously.

"Good. Well done," he answered, and handed her a cup of freshly brewed coffee.

"How was your trip?"

"The same."

"How is Sam?" She hid her jealousy of their close friendship and the fact that Sam had the opportunity to see her husband nearly every day.

"The same." Willis smiled.

"How are your courses?" she asked. Willis gave her a slightly amused, tired, yet impatient look. "Let me guess ... the same."

They sipped their coffee in silence. The first conversation was over, and there likely wouldn't be many more to follow. They never spoke about anything meaningful. They existed together for a few days each month with the demands of a baby dangling at the edge of every quiet minute. He finished his cup, kissed her on the head, and collected his suitcase to take to the bedroom. It was a joke that they continued to share the same bed. Nothing ever happened there. Perhaps there remained a hope of something happening. The bed was expertly made with the creases smoothed, linen sheets turned down, and pillows fluffed. He wondered if she slept beneath the covers or if she lay on top and waited for him. He placed his suitcase on the foot of the bed, making an imprint, and retrieved his reading assignments. Then he left the room and made a beeline for his small den. This was his routine, and she knew where to find him. She wouldn't intrude. Instead, she would soon start dinner. They had their own rooms where they didn't have to face any confrontation with themselves or each other; a familiar place in an imaginary home.

Chapter 22

Over the next couple of years, Willis Sr. painted a smile on his face. However, the paint was beginning to chip and crack. The completion of his law degree had gone much slower than planned, as he struggled to meet his assignment deadlines and catch up on the material he had missed while on hiatus. He had also received word from Ivy that his father had passed away. He wrote back to say that he couldn't leave this time to attend the funeral. Then he retreated into a long period of mourning. He was civil to his in-laws and wife and indifferent to his son as he looked ahead to his graduation and dreams of becoming a barrister. There was a cold clutch on his heart, and the only levity he found was in Sam, who was carefree and had no other personal attachments or conflicts. He and Sam were focused on the same future. They had discussed building a small firm together once they got their feet wet and gained a few client relationships and stronger credibility. Willis had been drifting away from family life for some time, and somehow, it became increasingly easier to become a ghost in his own home. Or were his wife and child the ghosts and he the living resident trying to expel them? In any fashion, they were living within different worlds that were hesitant to collide.

Finally, graduation day arrived, and more out of duty than pride, his family attended to witness his one great accomplishment. His in-laws frowned in their chairs while Ellie busied herself with Willis Jr., trying to get him to stop squirming in his seat. They clapped admirably when he appeared in the long march of law graduates, and Willis Jr. nearly jumped out of his seat yelling "Daddy! Daddy!" Willis Sr. gave them a short wave and broad smile. He was smiling at himself more than the people who had supported him to realize this end: the end of a long road of distance, intense focus, and sacrifice.

Sam trailed on his heels with his head held at a slightly higher angle, both of them once again marching into some vast and uncertain territory. He would have graduated sooner, but he took a short leave to help Willis get through his dark time and help with the baby as much as possible. He also had to catch up on his credits for his English literature classes to graduate in the same semester. As they looked toward the future, they both knew there would be challenges and dangers, steep inclines in their road of ambition. The light at the end of their tunnel was blinding and seductive. Once they walked through, it would be hard for anyone to follow.

After the grave speeches, delivery of the scrolls, and switching of tassels, there was a thunderous clapping in the theatre while Willis Sr. turned to his friend, Sam, and vigorously shook his hand.

"We've arrived," he said triumphantly. Two words that summed up a mountain of days. Sam returned the smile, his face almost bursting. Moments later, they left their throne-like seats and went to seek out their families. Willis Sr. was greeted with strong handshakes and pats on his shoulder from his in-laws and a demure kiss from his wife as his son clung to his leg. Their smiles were clearly painted on, although everyone agreed it was a great and long-awaited day. The family celebrated by going to an upscale pub restaurant and clanking pints of beer. Willis Jr. quietly sipped at an ice tea next to his mother and tried to not squirm in his seat. He was only two, but he knew the day was special. He listened quietly while his grandparents asked his daddy about his plans for being a successful barrister and how much competition he would face in the hiring market. After a while, the adult words only buzzed incoherently above his head as his mother continued to fuss over him.

Ellie only half-listened to her husband's enthusiasm. He never mentioned her in his plans for this new road to success. The only person he talked about was Sam. Her husband was completely oblivious to the subtle, wary glances that were exchanged between her parents, as their words masked their skepticism.

"That is wonderful, son, that you have a friend to help you start out on the right footing. We hope you two can make a go of it," Mr. Birch said. However, he didn't offer any more funds to help get them going, which Willis Sr. has been secretly hoping for, but it didn't matter. Sam and he had smarts and charisma; he was convinced they would go far. The two men had faced so much together already: enemy bullets, nail-biting exams, and personal setbacks. He knew they would see another victory.

As if by the mere mention of his name, Sam appeared in the restaurant a short while later. Willis Sr. eyed him first and waved him over. Ellie secretly wondered if this chance meeting was prearranged.

"Mom, dad," Willis Sr. started, "you remember my future partner." Sam shook hands with Ellie's parents and smiled broadly at Ellie and Willis Jr. Ellie smiled and promptly turned her attention back to her young son.

"Hi, Sam," Mrs. Birch said politely. "Congratulations to you both."

"Thank you; what a great day it is," replied Sam. "Sometimes old Willis and I thought we might not make it." He motioned fondly to his friend who was trapped in the back of the restaurant booth. Willis Sr. laughed heartily.

"Won't you join us, old man?" Willis Sr. coaxed his friend.

"Thanks, mate. My parents are waiting for me at our table, but I will come back after we've finished our drinks," Sam promised. He nodded to everyone and left the table.

After another pint, Ellie's parents began reaching for their coats and muttering about places they needed to be. Willis stood up and made a gesture to shake hands with his father-in-law. Mr. Birch hesitated for a second and then grabbed Willis' hand with one aggressive shake, saying, "Good job." Ellie turned to Willis and announced, "I'm going to get a lift with my parents. I'll meet you at home, darling." She swiftly picked up their little boy.

"Fine," Willis said. "See you at home." The small group left the table, paid at the counter, and shimmied out the door. They had each chipped in for Willis' lunch and drinks as well; a parting gift. Willis sighed and sat down at the empty table and finished his beer. Ironically, he was glad Ellie and Willis Jr. had left with her parents. The only disappointment was that he wanted to be the one to ask her to go home so he could visit with Sam. The way the situation had turned out, she was happily leaving him behind, which quietly annoyed him. He looked up to find Sam standing over him.

"They seemed to be happy for you," he said.

"Yeah," Willis replied. "Too bad they hate me."

"Well, can you really blame them, mate. You haven't exactly been the model husband." Sam sat down.

"I've been working damn hard at making something of myself. Ellie should understand that."

"... At the cost of losing her, though? No wife can be so alone for that long."

"So now you're full of advice. Nice timing."

"I'm your friend, mate. I'm just here to tell it like it is. I don't mean to pull you in one direction or another. Whatever you think you need to do, I'm here for support."

"Some friend," Willis muttered. Sam was right, though. He wouldn't have listened if Sam told him to cut down on his courses or try to work things out at home. He was set on his path. "Okay, thanks, Sam."

"Just saying it like it is." Sam shrugged.

"So, your parents must be proud today," Willis said. He wanted to shift gears.

"Ecstatic. My mother never thought I would make it, so she told me." Sam grinned from ear to ear. "I have an idea, mate, if you're up for it."

"What's that?"

"I believe we deserve some relaxation time. How would you like to take off with me for a few days in Paris?"

"We haven't been over there since the service. It would be nice to enjoy the city," Willis mused. He thought of his wife and how eager she was to leave him with the last few drops of his beer. She may have missed him before, but she clearly wasn't missing him now. "Sure, why the hell not?"

"Swell!" Sam exclaimed. "How about we leave next Friday?"

"Sounds swell." Willis grinned.

"Paris?" Ellie said. "You want to go to Paris with Sam?"

"Yes," Willis replied flatly. "I want to go to Paris with Sam."

"You just graduated after six years of living at Cambridge. You've been home for less than a week. Now you want to pack your bag again and go off running around Paris with Sam."

"It's been difficult, Ellie. We deserve a break."

"Difficult? Mmm. *You* deserve a break?" Ellie planted her feet in the bedroom carpet.

"Yes," Willis replied again. "Jesus, are you going deaf?" He unfastened his tie and threw it on the bed. Ellie looked at him for an uncomfortably long time. She looked at him until she didn't seem to see him anymore.

"That's fine, Willis. You go to Paris with Sam." She tossed her basket of folded laundry on the bed and left the room, closing the door soundly behind her. He watched her go.

Two days later, Sam arrived outside the flat at dawn in his new Morris Minor. He tapped the horn. Ellie appeared half-concealed in the upstairs window like a phantom as Willis bounded out the front door. He didn't turn around to wave goodbye to his wife.

"Let's go," Willis said.

"Did you say goodbye to your kid?" Sam asked.

"He's still asleep," Willis replied and casually threw his bag in the backseat. Sam pulled away from the suburban curb. The car seemed to float on top of the road as Willis sank into the passenger seat.

"Okay, mate?" Sam asked.

"I need this."

"I believe you do. You need to take care of yourself," Sam said. The two men travelled along the freeway to Dover with the hum of the motor speaking for them. When they did talk, the conversation turned toward their plans of starting a law firm together. They congratulated each other on their academic achievements and looked to the future with high hopes. Willis felt he had escaped, if only for a four-day weekend. Soon, they reached the ferry terminal. Sam parked the car and turned off the engine. The men unloaded their bags and walked away from the car. They would be crossing over to Paris on foot, in their thin-soled shoes. They would be wanderers.

For this time, Willis had no wife and no son. He would be Sam's equal. He would be divorced from his other life by a body of water, the English Channel: his available mistress. She was there waiting, always. Willis leaned on the boat's railing with the sea air beating his eyelids and the flaps of his jacket, watching her body rise and fall beneath him all the way to Calais.

Chapter 23

The coast was grey, and the sea was choppy as the ferry rode into the French port. When they finally arrived on shore, as the waves seemed to keep pushing them back, they boarded the train to Paris. Willis sunk into a solemn mood and gazed out the window for the duration of the trip, not seeing the scenic countryside. He couldn't stop thinking about Ellie. Partly, he was mad at her for giving in so easy. Once again, he was left with the feeling that the decision had not been his to make—she simply allowed him to go. She had dismissed him. She used to rage and cry and stomp her feet. He hated it, but he enjoyed the fact that she cared. Now she was hollow and cold. Her passion was gone; for him and for her paintings. Since she had given birth to Willis Jr., she hadn't bothered to try to reclaim her figure, and each time he came home from Cambridge, he was bombarded with her nattering and concerns about the state of their home and the baby. She had nothing spare to give him, no shred of affection. He wanted her to pine for him like she had during all of the time he was away at war, fighting for their future and freedom. Now *that* Ellie seemed to be lost and gone. Perhaps she had even taken a lover. Perhaps his son wasn't even his son. The thought jabbed him in his right temple as he rubbed his knuckles against his mouth.

In the beginning of the trip, Sam tried to make light conversation. Now he had given up and sat across the way reading a newspaper. There was no use in consulting his friend, Willis thought. Sam would only tell him everything he already knew, or thought he knew; he would only tell him the same as before: *he may not be a shining example of a husband, but he also needed to make himself happy*. Sam's words rang in his head and blocked out his self-pity. He realized that Ellie deserved happiness too. He wasn't thinking of divorce, just change. She was happy raising their son, and he was happy building his career. So what if they didn't meet in the middle as often? He would try to keep the machine of their marriage running and all of the loose nuts and bolts in check. Perhaps it was rickety, but it wouldn't fall apart. He wouldn't let it. He shrugged and looked at his watch. "Almost there," he said.

When the train reached Paris, the sky had cleared. Or it was a different sky. Enough time had gone by since the war for Paris to recover from its structural damage. Still, there was a lingering oppression in the air. The people were more guarded. They shuffled by with averted eyes. Paris before the devastation would have music and buskers in the streets. The two friends walked along the Seine, close together, tipping their hats cordially to the passersby with a quiet "bonjour." In return, they were given suspicious glances—*English? American? German?* There was no way of knowing without a uniform. Willis and Sam briefly stopped to browse in a tourist shop. Willis picked up a miniature Eiffel Tower.

"I think Willis Jr. would like this, don't you?" he asked Sam casually. He talked about his son as though he was someone else's junior. Sam grimaced.

"I think he would rather you bring him with you," he answered.

"Oh, Sam, you know I can't do that," Willis said briskly. "He's too young to appreciate everything Paris has to offer. Besides, he would probably grow tired and bored and spend the entire time talking about his mother."

"I suppose you're right," Sam said.

"Sam, I don't have Cambridge anymore," Willis continued. "I need a place that is mine, a place that isn't connected to my wife. I have Paris, and I have you." He wanted to say that he needed an escape, but he didn't dare. Escape implied a weakness, a need to run away.

"I understand," Sam said. They walked on and found a pub and then a few more. By the time they entered pub number four, they were feeling no pain. They chose a table inside and near the back. Willis noticed an attractive waitress approaching their table, and as she got closer, he blinked through his beer vision. She looked familiar, but he couldn't place her. Then she spoke. Her voice tripped lightly over her words with a muddled accent. She smiled easily and carried herself as though lifted by a breeze. They ordered a pitcher of the house beer. As she left the table, Willis cautiously mouthed her name, "Frieda." It was barely a whisper, but loud enough for her to hear. She turned around slowly, standing beside the table, incredulous, with the small pad of paper trembling in her hand. She squinted at him and slowly her mouth stretched into a smile.

"Willis?" she said. Sam sat back in amazement.

"What are you doing here?" Willis asked. Suddenly, he was embarrassed that he was drunk.

"Working," she laughed. "And you?" She had a strong urge to sit down next to him in the booth, but knew her boss would reprimand her on the spot. She could get fired if she talked to the customers for too long.

"Visiting," he answered. "Um, do you remember my friend Sam?"

"Why should she remember me?" Sam cut in.

"I do, vaguely," Frieda replied. Her cheeks were turning pink.

"You cut your hair," Willis commented. She sported a stylish chin-length bob.

"Yes," she said. Her hand smoothed her hair self-consciously.

"I like it," Willis said. She smiled, looking more relaxed. She looked young and fresh, yet poised and independent. He couldn't imagine Ellie with short hair, and he would probably be upset if she did cut it. He would think of it as an act of rebellion. Frieda could pull it off, though. Somehow, with Frieda it was a different story.

"Would you like to meet me here later?" she asked. Willis nodded.

"Of course," he said. She walked away to fetch their pitcher.

Chapter 24

ELLIE

Ellie lived a secret life. Her son was now a toddler, a little person who was able to move about freely. She remembered how dependent he used to be and how she could barely move a foot without him hanging from her breast. Those broken sleeps and long days interrupted by crying, cooing, and suckling. She had felt like a walking milk carton that never seemed to expire. If she did, her son didn't care. As long as she was able and available when he needed her. Strangely, she missed those days. Her son had helped fill the gaping hole that was left by her husband's absence. Sometimes she cried quietly in the early morning darkness, while her son obliviously continued to suck out her essence. She thought every drop might have been taken and that her mind was turning to milk as well. Her only salvation was her son's smile, and her painting. While nursing, she longed for the canvas. At times, she felt guilty about allowing her mind to wander to the evocative images that appeared before her in the middle of the night. Still, she hung on to them with tenacity and saved them for when her son would nap during the daytime.

As soon as he was asleep, she would lay him in the safety of his crib, a little jail, and steal away to the spare room she had fashioned with stripped hardwood floors and drop cloths where her mind awaited freedom. She would open the curtains hanging on the small window and let in the world. Her husband thought her paintings were forgotten and collecting dust like the cobwebs in the corners. She once almost told her husband that she kept the spark of her inspiration, but before she managed to let him in, he told her she was killing herself and that her paintings were dying. He had hurt her, so she decided not to tell him about how she was keeping them alive, all of them. She hid them away in a large closet when he came home. She had not forgotten, not with one breath. Instead, she lived in her paintings. She lived every day, despite her dark, broken nights and swollen breasts. She lived for herself and her son. Her husband was only a phantom who visited them, haunting them. They had learned to pay little attention to him: the silent, infrequent stranger in their home. Sadly, she watched her son try to vie for his father's attention, only to be shooed away and told to behave. She would give her son cookies afterwards and wipe away the tears that brimmed on the edges of his sky blue eyes.

In her studies at Cambridge, she had learned the classical technique of painting and would try to mimic the world exactly as it appeared. She had painted landscapes and portraits with a delicate hand, drawing every minute detail and filling in the spaces with appropriate colours. The trees were green in the summer and filled with bright colours in the autumn. The sky was blue or grey or touched with purple and orange sunsets. The clouds were white and the sun was yellow. Every touch of paint to the canvas had a purpose.

Now the paint deviated from the lines. Nothing was contained. The paint flew across the large canvases with large, brave strokes. She would often paint her husband. She would paint him handsome. She would paint him angry. She would paint both of them with their mouths open, devouring one-third of their faces. She would paint her breasts over and over, because they had a story of their own to tell. Her breasts had their own evolution. Sometimes she yelled while she spilled her true colours: black suns and purple trees, dark faces and a hint of light somewhere in the background. The light seemed to draw in the dark, a spark of quiet hope. The chaos of colour seemed to spiral around the light, never getting there. There was no clear path, no place of certainty to attract the eye. These paintings exhausted her, but in the end she would feel emptied of all desperation. The canvas ate her sadness. She had better days, when bars of sunlight on the floor would make her stay within the lines, a more conventional place. She would paint with a calm hand on those days: a blur of bright-coloured flowers, just out of focus, and dabs of green leaves and cream-coloured clouds. She would make the sun orange again, a burning ball of new energy. The once-blank canvases stood stacked against the walls around her, a growing testimony and jury: a record of her life and muse in marriage and motherhood.

Chapter 25

A few hours later, Willis returned to the pub expecting Frieda to be finished with her shift. If she wasn't ready, he could have a drink while he waited. He left Sam at the hotel room with a deck of cards and the mini bar. Walking down to meet her, he couldn't help noticing the familiarity of the situation. It seemed they had both been circling around and around in their lives only to return back to this same spot. When he entered the pub, he spotted her in the back, hastily untying her apron. She caught sight of him and flashed her smile. They walked out into the evening together, arm in arm. No time had passed between them.

"I thought about you," she blurted out.

"Oh, me too," he said eagerly. There was no need for awkwardness and, sadly, no time to be wasted.

"I knew you would survive the war," she said. "Are you a big-shot lawyer now?" He smiled at her. She had remembered everything.

"I just graduated from law school," he beamed. "Sam and I are going to start a law practice together."

"That is wonderful."

"Why are you living in Paris?" he asked.

"You mean why did I not stay in Holland?" she said.

"Yes—I mean, isn't that your home?"

"It was," she replied softly. "I'm not sure I have a home anymore. Everything is so different now. My father's homeland is also divided, in every way." The Berlin Wall had severed the lives of the German people. Many families will possibly never see each other again.

"The people won't forget," she continued. "We knew it would only get worse. Perhaps, one day, when the memory of the war has faded, I will go there." She shrugged. "My father will probably never return to Germany."

"Why not?" Willis asked. She looked at him like he was a naïve child.

"He may be shunned for deserting his native home, for not standing strong with his countrymen. He never subscribed to Hitler's notion of creating a better Germany by securing world domination. My father views the world as one large village—he has a soft, visionary heart," she sighed. "My father's attempt to flee involvement in the war was in vain. The Germans still made him a prisoner in his newfound country."

"Yes, but it's all over now. It's been over for years. I'm sure your father can return one day if he chooses to," Willis offered. He wanted to say that he was sure many German people shared her father's ideas of a peaceful world and that they were most likely also relieved the war had ended and Hitler was gone. Somehow, it seemed fruitless to say so. Even after all these years, the wounds were still fresh for all those who had been affected by the war. Families had been ripped apart and lives demolished; it was hard to forget the past, no matter how many decades ago it happened. It still happened.

"That may be so," Frieda sighed, "but who wants to live in a place where they can't be who they are? It is a prison to live with thoughts and ideas that must be kept secret."

"Where do you live?" he asked, changing the subject.

"I'm taking you there."

Chapter 26

Willis rolled over in Frieda's single-cot bed and smoothed her short, tousled hair behind her ear.

"I dreamed of this," she said.

"Did you?" he mused sleepily. He pulled the bed sheets toward him. "Why don't you have a bigger bed?"

"I don't need one. It's just me, silly," she said and lightly smacked him on the head.

"Oh?" he was genuinely surprised.

"I don't need men to fill the cracks in my life. Men just take up time," she said.

"Well, in that case—I'll just go," Willis pretended to get out of the bed, but she arrested him with her arms.

"Not so fast," she said. "Your time isn't up yet." He kissed her, hard. When she came up for air she looked at him pointedly. "So, what happened to you?" she asked.

"What do you mean?"

"Well ... did you get married?"

Willis rolled away from her with a long sigh, folding his arms to make a pillow behind his head. "Yes, I got married."

"Do you love her?" She looked away from him.

"She's my wife."

"That isn't an answer."

"Okay, then. The truth is—I don't know anymore," he said. "I never dreamed I would see you again. I mean, I didn't think it was possible."

"I believe we make things possible," she said. She sounded so sweet, it made him ache. They lay together for a long time, not wanting to think about the past or the future. Finally, she hoisted herself on her side with her naked breast brushing his side and her inquisitive eyes hovering over him. "How long will you stay in Paris?" she asked.

"A few days," he answered. She nodded, trying to make sense of their chance encounter.

"When will you come back to Paris?"

"As soon as I can," he replied.

"Good," she said.

Willis called the hotel to tell Sam that he would spend the day with Frieda. Sam, of course, gave him a mild guilt trip about how the trip was meant for them to get away and discuss the law practice and not for a romantic rendezvous. In the end, Sam relented and said he would meet Willis the next day. He envied his friend's happiness and took a quiet vow of discretion. He remembered how lovesick and tortured Willis had been the first time he left Frieda behind. Now she had come back into his life like a shining light, and there was no war to tear them away from their found happiness. Sam refused to be a barrier that would separate or diminish what was meant to be, even for this short time. There were enough complications. If it didn't work, then it would be by their doing.

Willis had checked out of the hotel and brought his suitcase to Frieda's flat, which was small and bright with sparse furniture and decor. She had been living in the same flat since she moved to Paris shortly after the war ended. She didn't want to accumulate too many possessions, or become too attached, in case she decided to leave. She never intended to settle anywhere. She felt like a foreigner in her own skin. Willis gave her one more reason to stay in Paris, although he didn't know when he would be able to return.

Willis didn't want to create further tension or raise any suspicion at home. Despite the dissatisfaction in his marriage, he had a wife and child, and he wasn't going to break apart his family. He refused to be "that man" who risked too much, only to lose everything. He told Frieda as much, and she insisted that she didn't want to disrupt his life. Even so, they both knew it was already done. On his last night with Frieda, they made love gently. She was careful not to cling to him, although she pressed her body close. She wanted to leave her scent on him. She wanted him to take a part of her home to his wife and child. She wanted to stay in his veins.

Chapter 27

When Willis returned to London with Sam, the Channel was even choppier. The two friends made small talk, speaking of nothing important. Sam had visited the tourist sights while his friend reclaimed a near-extinguished flame in Frieda's bed. Ellie met her husband on the other side, which unnerved Willis. He plastered on a tolerant smile and greeted his wife with a peck on the cheek. Willis Jr. was in the backseat of the car, anxiously awaiting his father's arrival. Willis handed his son the small Eiffel Tower.

"Did you go away, Daddy?" his son asked.

His father didn't answer. They drove home, subdued and each caught up in their own mind chatter. Life at home continued at its usual speed, like a well-worn machine. The events and conversations were predictable, and Willis focused his energy on starting the law practice with Sam. At least once a month he travelled to Paris on his own. In the beginning, Sam accompanied his friend a few times, to uphold the charade for Ellie, but soon, he chose to hold down the fort at the office instead. Willis told his wife that there were potential clients in Paris who wanted to meet with him and that he was travelling to drum up business and increase networking opportunities. Ellie didn't ask questions, although she silently wondered why he couldn't network more on British soil. She kept the house clean, made the meals, and took care of their son.

On one particular trip to Paris, after a year of travelling back and forth, Willis tumbled onto Frieda's bed with his usual sense of relief, desire, and exhaustion. He had just arrived and looked at her, puzzled that she remained in the doorway.

"Come here, sweetheart." He patted the bed cover. "What is it?"

She hesitated and looked as though she might back out of the room and run in the other direction. "I'm pregnant," she said with a sob breaking in her throat. Willis suddenly felt his stomach drop, as though he had just come out of an elevator that plummeted. Willis and Frieda's visit was sober as they tried to discuss the severity of the situation they were facing, the ramifications. She was excited as well, but she kept her enthusiasm in check, because she knew what it would mean to Willis, how it would place extra pressures on his life. However, she didn't have a very convincing poker face. At one point during their visit, he took her hand and led her to the couch.

"This isn't bad news," he said gently.

"But—your family," she began. He put a finger over her lips.

"You're my family too," he said calmly. "Legally, you should have been my family." Their lives were like the jumbled pieces in a kaleidoscope glass, tossed around and changing shape. He wished he didn't want to be with her so much. He wished he'd been more careful, more patient. He wished for so many things, except what was happening now.

Over the following months, during his infrequent visits, he could tell she was excited about the baby, full of nervous anticipation, as any first-time mother should be. He didn't want to take that away from her. Early on in her pregnancy, she made the bold decision to move back to Germany. She told Willis it was time—she didn't want to run from her father's past any longer. She wanted her baby to be born in his homeland. Willis supported her decision and helped her make the necessary arrangements to travel and secure a modest apartment in Lüneburg to begin her new life. He cringed slightly at the notion of having to travel farther to be with her, but in the same heartbeat, he was glad that she was moving herself farther away from him. In the beginning, he continued to tell Ellie that he was making connections in France; however, as the additional travel made his stays longer, he extended his lie by telling her that his networking opportunities reached farther into the continent. He was vague and she no longer asked him where he was going or how long he was staying away, which also stung him.

When Frieda was six months along, finally enjoying the blooming roundness of her tummy and the fluttering movements, and not running to the bathroom every hour, he was already trying to find a solution. He felt guilty secretly thinking about how to mend his own life when their child wasn't even born yet. The truth was that he didn't know how much longer he could continue leading two separate lives. He wasn't being fair to Frieda or Ellie, and he also had Willis Jr. to think about. He was failing everyone, and it would only get worse. He had thought of his estranged sister, Ivy. She hadn't written to him since his father's passing, or even before then, in the years she'd been living in his neck of the woods. He often wondered why she had no children or if she had a child now. If not, *perhaps it was because she didn't want to have babies*, he thought. There were enough people in the world already. He was quietly defending his sister, and the thought didn't run through his mind without notice. She was quiet and somewhat prudish, but she was also practical. Although it wasn't clear whether his sister couldn't or wouldn't bear the fruit of children in her marriage, he still had a niggling thought that she might be an answer to his dilemma. She and her husband were an affluent couple: their unborn child wouldn't want for anything. He pushed the idea out of his head for a while. It wasn't time. Perhaps there would never be the right time. He needed to be there for Frieda and not let on that he wanted to rid himself of this coming burden. Who was he? He wasn't this cold; sadly, he was trapped and married to the wrong woman. Could there be some way to escape? Some portal to disappear into and escape his two lives that were both heading toward broken bridges?

Willis was torn, yet also secretly relieved when Frieda confronted him two years later with an ultimatum. She told him that she couldn't endure raising their son on her own—it was too difficult, and she wanted Willis Sr. to be permanently in their lives. She wanted him to make a clear decision, but she did not prepare herself for the outcome. Willis was not going to leave his wife and young son. Frieda was surprised when he proposed giving their son to his sister, Ivy. In her vulnerable state, she realized she couldn't go on watching their son grow, having him as a daily reminder of his father, the man she could never truly keep. She wanted all or nothing—as painful as the decision was and how much it stabbed at her heart. His biting words echoed in her mind: *I can't do this anymore either.* Her plan had backfired, and she couldn't back down now; she couldn't show him her weakness. She didn't want him to know how intensely she loved him and how much she would sacrifice for him, especially since he was leaving anyway. It was clear there was nothing she could do to make him stay.

Willis was equally surprised and strangely disappointed by how easily she gave in and was willing to give away their son; although it was a convenient resolution for him, he questioned her scruples and the depth of her heart. She was throwing away their one true bond of blood and family, such as it was. She complained about how she was incapable of caring for him any longer by herself; she said she felt ill-equipped and needed his emotional support. She needed him to be a constant. Willis sufficiently provided for them so they could live relatively comfortably. However, he knew his end of the bargain came up short. Still, he wanted to point out to her that she was a grown woman and it was childish and selfish of her to consider abandoning her son, but he would be throwing stones in a glass house. He was as much to blame, wanting to rid himself of the responsibility for a human life that should have completed a perfect family for him. This boy was an unwitting part of the wrong triangle. The connected dots couldn't lead back to Willis—he had to construct a trapdoor to remove himself or one of the incriminating pieces from this false life. He had to unravel this sordid mess—light the match and forget it.

IVY

When Willis had enlisted in the Canadian forces, Ivy's world became a little bit smaller. She was a mouse—in her appearance and personality—small, quiet, uninteresting, but there was a universe happening inside of her that no one knew. She and Willis had never been close, but he was her brother, an ally, a gateway to the world. He was popular and often brought his school buddies over to the house. Of course, they never noticed her, but she silently watched them from behind corners. She didn't fancy his friends, but she wanted to belong. When he left their house for good, life with her parents became suffocating. If she felt isolated before, it was nothing compared to having two small-minded parents who didn't expect much from her or encourage her to do anything beyond what their small town expected, which was to marry and start pumping out kids. She was more similar to her younger brother than anyone realized, or perhaps wanted to admit. She did want to marry and have children, but she also wanted to become something more important, to have something that was hers alone.

She secretly wrote short stories about people in other places and imagined herself in their shoes. She worked in the post office. Most of the mail was domestic, but there was the odd letter or package destined for some exotic place across the ocean. She tended to hold them a second too long before placing them in the mail sorter for pick-up or delivery. One day, long after the war ended, a British gentleman sauntered in to the post office and struck up a conversation with her. He was a self-proclaimed entrepreneur who was visiting Canada looking for networking opportunities. A month later, the two were married and Ivy was on a boat to England to start a new adventure with her husband, and she thought, *caution be damned*.

Ivy's womb was a dark cave. In that place, the beginnings of children sparked, formed, and dissipated like small, bursting stars; the tiny remains of what and who they might have been floated back into the ether, becoming one with everything else. Ivy died, too, over and over again.

Ivy stood shaking in the doorway that was opened only wide enough for her brother to poke his head in. She was holding a cigarette and puffed on it absentmindedly. He had called her a few days earlier, a warning of sorts. He didn't delve into all of the details on the telephone—he had wanted to ask her in person. She watched him cautiously and knew from the tone of his voice on the phone that he wanted to discuss serious business. She hadn't spoken to him since her mother's funeral, and she was still sore that he didn't come through to be with her after their father's passing. Besides not having the emotional support of her brother, he had also left her to handle all of the funeral and burial arrangements. Now he was on her doorstep, looking desperate and anxious. Suddenly, she seemed to be the one in a position of power: the rescuer, the keeper at the manger. She was a shell of a woman, living in the shadowed luxury of her husband, who provided well for her but was rarely home. He was away slaying dragons and chasing down pots of gold, trying to make something out of nothing. Fortunately, he somehow managed to come home with new prospects and money in his pockets. He was charismatic and intelligent, and she counted herself lucky in that regard.

"Hello, Ivy," Willis began, painfully aware that they had to create a beginning. Their conversations would start up from a long, lonely pause; they could not blame it on busy lives or pretend to have any reference of where to start again. They were strangers, lost from childhood.

"Hello, Willis." She made no motion to invite him in, but instead opened the door a bit wider and leaned purposefully over the threshold. "You sounded urgent on the phone. Whatever could be the matter?" Her tone was biting.

"May I come in?" It wasn't a question. It was a plea. She hesitated and then moved away from the door. She walked toward her expensive couch, slowly and deliberately, like a cougar, or a drunken woman who was trying very hard to conceal it. She was polished: no more awkwardness or blushing. He realized that he wasn't merely estranged from her; he didn't know her at all. The fact hit him like a block of ice. Sadly, maybe it would be easier this way. He couldn't carry on with his two existences. She had the means to raise his son, and he would never need to be a part of his life or add any confusion or pain to an already difficult situation. He hoped she would give his son enough warmth to keep him safe and on a straight and healthy track. It was the best option he could hope for: blood keeping blood. Then he could vanish behind the curtains. He sat down beside her lightly on the far end of the couch.

"I have a delicate situation. I have a mistress and a two-year-old son that shouldn't have been born. She insisted on naming him Willis," he said. Ivy's right eyebrow spiked, as she knew of his older son. Willis continued hastily, "But you can change his name to whatever you want."

"Me?" The twist in the story had come too soon. She was getting swept up in her quiet happiness hearing about his unfortunate circumstances, until she suddenly felt dragged down in his whirlpool.

"I thought of you and your husband," he went on, hardly breaking his stride, "you seem to be prominent citizens: married, wealthy, successful. I know you don't have children. Wouldn't you like to have a child, Ivy? You have softness in you—you always have. I know I teased you endlessly when we were younger. Isn't that what brothers are supposed to do? I'm sorry—" He stopped suddenly, noticing the strangled expression on her face. She was visibly fighting back tears.

"You should go," she began. He wasn't going to give up that easily.

"Would you raise my son for me? For us?" he was kneeling on the floor, despite himself. "I won't come around anymore afterwards. I promise. I don't ever want him to know. He needs a stable home. He needs a chance. We can't give him what he needs. We're not strong enough." He watched her take a long drag from her cigarette, feeling his heart tearing in his chest. He didn't want to upset her any further, so he simply gave her his number. She looked at the digits on the small paper as though they were hieroglyphics she was attempting to decipher. She had a curious, concentrated look on her face. Finally, she said, "I'll consider it. However, I do need you to go now." Willis nodded and quietly showed himself out.

The room was suddenly empty. In his wake, he left his problems and filled the space with a heaviness that was only just beginning to lift for Ivy, the dense presence of partially-formed, unborn babies. Her husband would be home the next morning, so she had the night to weigh in her own mind, her own heart, if she could suffer to raise a child that did not come from her. Furthermore, could she ethically agree to provide for the child of her estranged, selfish, arrogant younger brother, whose luck had finally caught up with him? But, in all fairness, the traits of her brother were not to be burdened by his illegitimate son. The night would be long; the morning could bring the birth of a new world.

A week later, Ivy phoned her brother. She had spent several sleepless nights wondering if her heart could stretch enough to love and provide for someone else's child. She was also hesitant to propose the idea to her husband, but was astonished to find that when she did muster up the nerve to ask him, he was overjoyed by the prospect of having a son. Maybe that was all he cared about, the idea of having someone to continue his name. So she pushed her doubts aside and relented to the notion as well. When her brother answered the phone, all she could say was "Alright, Willis." Her hand on the receiver was shaking uncontrollably and she wasn't sure why. She knew the magnitude of what she was saying in that one small word, but she was not overwhelmed by excitement; instead, she felt her stomach turning. She had not allowed herself to feel so physically upset since her last miscarriage. In this moment, instead of anticipating the gift of a child, she felt as though she was giving much more of herself away. She was accepting a fate that she had not wanted, not if it didn't come from her own flesh. She was appeasing the men in her life. Still, she had managed to utter that small word, a lie that would alter everything—"Alright."

Willis made the difficult arrangements to transport his son from Frieda's arms to his new home with his sister and her husband in London. Sam travelled back from Lüneburg with Willis Sr., at his request, and held the boy so that people would think the young child belonged to him in some fashion should they be confronted by any acquaintances. When they reached Ivy's home, the child was tired and cranky, displaying all his vices of the "terrible twos." Upon meeting him, Ivy cringed visibly. She spoke to the boy as though he were beyond his years, telling him to "smarten up." Then she swiftly bore the child in her arms, gave her brother an unwavering look, and said, "I won't tell him the truth, but I won't lie either. We will adopt him and he can have my husband's last name, but I refuse to pretend to be his mother. He will know me as his aunt, and the rest I won't divulge. You and your mistress will become ghosts, do you understand?" Willis nodded dumbly. He immediately felt more edgy about leaving his son with her, but the situation was hopeless. He sucked in his breath, gave the boy a short, heartfelt hug, planted a firm kiss on the top of his head, and turned to leave with Sam, whose gaze lingered a moment longer, sending a silent message to Ivy—with imploring, soulful eyes—to be kind to the boy. She closed the door, tight-lipped, with the boy crying in her arms.

The long years that followed ate away at Willis, haunting him like a reaper. He remained married to Ellie, but only on paper. In all aspects of his life, it seemed he had become a ghost after all. He appeared briefly for whatever pressing matter summoned him, predominately in his career as he built a successful law firm from the ground up with Sam, and then, during the undemanding hours, he slinked away into the shadows—his small library at home, familiar taverns, or the company of convenient women—to hide and forget.

Many years later, a man in his seventies, a shadow of Willis Sr., sat at a desk in a dark room. Next to him was a small bottle of medication for his heart and a glass of whisky. He pulled an executive pen from inside his jacket and proceeded to write on a large white napkin. Then he folded the napkin in half and slipped it into an envelope. Next, he reached for the small bottle, unscrewed the cap, and poured half of the pills into his palm. He held them there for a moment, contemplating them.

"I failed, Dad. I failed everyone," he said into the dark. Then he casually scooped the pills into his mouth and chased them down with a long swig of whisky. He laid his head on the table and closed his eyes, anticipating a long and painless sleep.

After the funeral, Ellie returned from the cemetery in her husband's limousine, dressed in a black suit and wearing black satin gloves. She climbed the stairs to her flat and, in the front hallway, frowned at her reflection in the mirror. She took a nude-coloured lipstick from her purse and applied it to her aging lips. She then took a large, white napkin out of her hand purse, her hand shaking. The napkin was the only item left to her by her husband. She had read the napkin over and over since the morning when she had received it from Sam. She unfolded the napkin and read again the block letters in black ink:

DEAREST ELLIE—
I WAS NEVER FAIR TO YOU. FORGIVE ME.

She was told the napkin was found beside him, his final note. Ellie pressed her lips together on a corner of the napkin, visibly disturbed. She looked at the wastebasket, but folded the napkin carefully and placed it back in her purse. She closed the clasp smartly.